THE GUARDIAN OF WHISPERS

To Stephanie,

Ba Pidgett

THE REED BROTHERS AND

The Guardian of Whispers

A novel by

B. E. PADGETT

ISBN: 9798632008990

Cover design by: B. E. Padgett
Library of Congress Control Number: 2018675309
Printed in the United States of America

DEDICATION

To Mackenzie. Auntie loves you.

The Reed Family

CHAPTER 1

"Jon, he can't see us, can he?" Franklin whispered.

The twins peered through the bushes they were kneeling inside. There--pacing the yard with a grumpy scowl was Eugene. His brownish curls laying over his eyes as he squinted in their direction then peered away.

"No, he can't see us," Jon said. It was a hot day in southern Florida—upper nineties at least—and he pulled at the collar of his space t-shirt to let some fresh air travel down his chest.

"Good." Franklin wiped his own sweating forehead, and the branches swished with his movement. "What is our plan of action?"

Jon rubbed his chin as he focused on their target: the soccer ball on the patio table. The ball had been swiped from them an hour ago and now it was being held captive by the meanest of captors—Eugene, their older brother. "We need a distraction."

"How about Shakes?"

Across the yard, Shakes, their golden retriever, was sniffing behind a shrub.

"Good idea, Frank." The distraction would be easy, but they needed an entry strategy. Jon's eyes traveled to a low-hanging branch above the table, and a smirk touched his lips. Shoving a hand into his back pocket, Jon retrieved his Swiss army knifeCarefully, he cut a couple limbs from the bush they were hiding in and stuffed them into his backpack. "All right, I have a plan."

Frank gave him a look. "Why do I get the feeling I'm not going to like it much?"

"Don't be a wimp," Jon whispered as he pulled his pack onto his back and gave Frank a little shove.

They kept to the edge of the lawn, crushing the crab grass under their sandals until they reached the mango tree. It was tall for a mango tree, but despite its height and width, the branches hung only a few feet over the patio table.

The brothers creeped around the trunk, and Jon helped Frank climb into the dense branches, trying not to make noise. As soon as Frank reached the nearest stable branch, he twisted around to sit on it, lending a hand to help Jon up. Below their perch, Eugene was still eyeing the bush line some distance away.

Putting a finger to his lips, Jon grabbed a rock and slingshot out of his back pocket. He closed one eye and took aim for the far-left fence.

The rock shot forward and hit its mark. Eugene's concentration shifted, and he walked in the direction of the sound.

This was their chance.

Jon yanked a branch out of his backpack. He whistled, and Shakes's ears perked up, his tongue sloshing out of his mouth in excitement. The dog watched intently as Jon waved the stick above the mango tree leaves—he was not going to let the stick out of sight until it was in his mouth.

"Just throw it!" Frank said through clenched teeth as he scooted into position, moving one leg so he was sitting sideways on the branch.

Jon tossed the stick high in the air with all his strength. It twirled and twirled until landing—*thunk*—right into the overfilled kiddy pool near Eugene.

The stick bobbed on top of the water, and Shake dashed toward it.

"Hurry, Frank, we don't have much time!" Jon whispered.

Frank swung himself upside-down from the mango tree—Jon hanging on tight to his legs—and stretched his arms for the soccer ball.

Splash. Shakes had made it to the pool.

"What the . . . ?" an angry voice yelled. "Stupid dog!"

"A little lower, Jon," Frank said, his voice strained and his face turning red.

Jon's hold on his brother tightened as he let him down a couple more inches. It was hard for him to get a good grip.

"No, Shakes . . . no! Don't!" Eugene yelled. Shakes was prancing in the kiddy pool and splashing water everywhere. He stopped to shake, showering Eugene.

"Frank!" Jon's own face was reddening as he clung to Frank's jeans. "I don't know how much longer I can hold on."

"I'm almost there!" Frank's fingers curled around the soccer ball. "Pull me up!"

Biting his lip, Jon grabbed a handful of Frank's shirt and tried to haul his twin into the tree again.

Frank put the ball under one of his armpits so he could grasp Jon's shoulder. "Don't let go, Jon!"

"You're really heavy . . ." Jon tugged desperately on Frank's shirt. "I don't know if I can—" His sweaty hands started to shake. A wave of nausea rolled in his stomach and he suddenly felt dizzy.

A shadowy image flashed through Jon's mind of Frank slipping out of his grasp and landing on the table below.

The image disappeared, and Jon blinked to clear his head. His grip on Frank started to slip.

"Jon, NO! You can't let me—"

"Boys! What are you doing?"

Startled, Jon let go of Frank's shirt. In the exact way he'd seen it in his mind, Frank fell the three feet onto the patio table.

Groaning, his twin shot an angry sneer at him.

"Frank!" Jon shouted. "I'm so sorry!"

"Franklin!" the woman who had interrupted them rushed over. "Are you all right? What were you doing?"

"I'm OK," Frank said, wincing a little as he propped himself up on his elbows.

"Auntie Gladys! Auntie Gladys!" Eugene ran up to them, soaked and dripping from his encounter with Shakes.

Jon jumped from the tree branch and kicked the soccer ball Frank had dropped.

"Gene, what happened to you?" Aunt Gladys asked.

"They were trying to get the soccer ball," Eugene pointed at the twins. "You told them they couldn't play with it, and I was making sure . . ."

"He was guarding it." Frank glared at Eugene.

"Yeah, Genie. Who put you in charge?" Jon added.

"Don't call me Genie!" Eugene grumbled, his fists clenching.

"All of you! Stop!" Aunt Gladys shouted to get their attention, and they immediately fell silent. She ran her hand through her short graying hair in frustration. "Now, Jonathan, give me the soccer ball."

Jon went to retrieve it and handed it to her reluctantly, and Aunt Gladys tucked it under her arm.

"Franklin, you are going to follow me into the kitchen. I'm going to put some ice on that shoulder so it doesn't bruise."

Frank nodded.

"And you, Eugene, head to the shower and get yourself cleaned up. You all just wait . . ." She paused for dramatic effect. "Just wait until your parents get home."

As Jon was about to depart, head hanging low, Aunt Gladys's finger appeared in front of his nose. "I know this was your idea, Jonathan. Don't think for one minute that I'll let that slip."

"Um, yes, Aunt Gladys." Jon never tried to keep secrets from his aunt. She could always pick out the culprit in their shenanigans—and it was usually him.

A tug at her long flowery skirt diverted Aunt Gladys's attention. "One moment, Clara," she said to the four-year-old girl at her side. "Now, see what you boys have done? I was trying to finish Clara's hair."

Clara's long, straight red hair was half-braided on the

left side. The right was still dangling and knotted. Jon's little sister looked at him but didn't say anything, which wasn't unusual. Clara never talked much.

Taking the young girl's hand, Aunt Gladys went back into the house.

"Look what you've done!" Eugene shouted at Jon, gesturing to Frank's bruised shoulder. "You need to be more careful."

∩⌐

Frank thought Eugene was being ridiculous. If only he would leave them alone. Instead he had to stomp on their fun. "I'm fine, Genie. It's just a bump. Besides, why don't you just play ball with us next time?"

"Yeah," Jon added, "you don't play games with us anymore. Scared we'll break you, Genie?"

"What? No . . . wait . . . don't call me Genie!" Eugene's face turned red, and he stomped into the house.

Frank and Jon followed him inside, laughing as he tripped over a pair of legs lying between the couch and coffee table.

"Ow!" said a small voice.

"Peter! What are you doing?" Eugene asked, shooting a glare back at the giggle fest behind him.

"Oh, nothing . . ." The small voice heaved a deep sigh. "Waiting for someone to remember I live here . . . someone to ask me to play with them."

"You are such a downer." Eugene shook his head and stumbled off toward his bedroom.

Frank walked over so he could fully see their eight-year-old brother sprawled out on the carpet, the back of his hand resting on his head, his other hand clutching a book to his chest.

"You know, Peter," Jon said, "as much as I hate to say it, Genie is right. You need to stop lying around and make some friends."

"I tried to make a friend at school yesterday," Peter answered in a monotone.

"What happened?"

"Well, I tried talking to this boy who sits next to me. I asked him about our reading assignment."

"Sounds like a good start." Frank sighed. "Peter, please get up. You can at least look at us when you talk."

Peter raised himself onto his elbows and pursed his lips together in a scowl. "Good? He ignored me all day at school." Peter flopped onto the floor again. "Wouldn't even look at me."

"Gosh, Pete, what'd you say to him?" Jon asked.

"I don't know. I asked him how he likes the book we're reading, what other books he likes, how much he reads each day, you know. The usual."

"Well, that's not so bad."

"I did get upset when he told me he didn't like reading! But who doesn't like reading?"

Frank tilted his head so he could see the book Peter was holding. He recognized the cover—an illustrated girl sitting on top of a pile books: *Matilda*.

"What is wrong with you, Pete?" Jon walked away; he wasn't a big reader unless it was a comic book. Frank turned to follow, Peter's voice echoing behind them.

"To be great is to be misunderstood. . . ."

Aunt Gladys was waiting for them, an ice pack in hand. The next several minutes were taken up with Aunt Gladys's lecture as Frank pressed the ice to his shoulder.

"What was going through your head, Franklin? Listening to your brother with his harebrained ideas—climbing trees, falling from trees—all for something you shouldn't be playing with in the first place!"

Great Aunt Gladys's hot temper could not be cooled with a simple "yes, Auntie" or "no, Auntie." Franklin struggled to keep a straight face as Jon silently mimicked their aunt's words and hand motions behind her back.

Something shuffled around in the other room, and Peter's voice called out, "Mom!"

"Mom!" both Frank and Jon yelled. Frank jumped from the kitchen counter and ran behind his brothers toward the front door.

"Franklin Aaron Reed, I am not done with you!" his aunt called after him.

Running feet pounded all over the house as Eugene and Clara rushed down the stairs, Eugene's hair still damp from his shower.

"Yes, I'm home!" Their mother tossed her messenger bag on the entry table as Clara latched on to her right leg and Peter to her left. She leaned in to kiss Frank on the forehead, her mass of curly red hair tickling his ear. He wrapped his arms around her waist, and she startled a little when his cool shoulder touched her skin. "Oh, cold arm there, Franky."

"Mom, you won't believe what happened today," Eugene said, but Peter was also talking, and their words were jumbling over each other. Their mother's smiling eyes darted back and forth between them, trying to follow along.

"Oh, good, Cece, you're home," Aunt Gladys said with relief. "They are trying my patience today. All of them."

"Uh-oh . . ." Their mother clicked her tongue. "No wonder I'm getting such an enthusiastic welcome. OK, all of you, give Mom some room." They pulled back, and she took a deep breath and straightened her dark brown leather jacket. Frank caught a glimpse of her police badge. He wished, for the millionth time, she would let him play with it.

"Did you catch any villains today?" Peter asked, and she

ruffled his hair.

"Always, baby. I'm always keeping you safe. Aunt Gladys, we're having company tonight. Do you think we can make room for one more?"

"I don't see why not. I already feed an army as it is." Aunt Gladys smirked.

"Company? Who's coming over, Cecelia?" a deep boisterous voice asked from behind her. Frank peered around his mother to see his father standing in the door.

"Harvey!" Their mother whirled around as the crowd of children attacked the incoming parent. Frank and Jon climbed all over their tall, slender dad, as usual. They'd often wrestle him to the ground until he undid his tie and cried for mercy.

"Hey, sweetie," Dad grunted, trying to shake off Eugene, whose arm was around his windpipe. "OK, OK, now, boys, Clara, I actually need to talk to your mom."

"Boys! Clara! You heard your father. Off!" When their aunt spoke, they all listened. With firm pressure to their shoulders, she guided them into the kitchen and closed the door behind them.

"I hate when they kick us out!" Jon pulled Frank to the closed kitchen door. "OK, new plan. Frank, you're the best at listening in."

It was true. Frank felt that sometimes, if he concentrated

enough, the voices he listened to got louder and clearer, almost as if they were whispering directly to him. It would cut in and out, leaving bits and pieces missing, but he was still better at this duty than the rest of his siblings.

"I don't think this is a good idea," Eugene said.

"Aren't you even a little curious?" Frank pressed his ear to the crack in the door. Eugene hummed his disapproval but still hung nearby to listen with them.

"All right," Frank said, trying to decipher the muffled conversation, "someone is definitely coming over for dinner. I couldn't hear the name. But Dad doesn't seem happy about it."

"Oh no." Jon rolled his eyes. "I hope it's not Mrs. Grinch."

"It's not Mrs. Grinch. It's Mrs. Finch," Eugene corrected him.

"I don't care what her name is. She's really mean and super boring."

"No, she isn't . . . well, yes, she is, but—"

"Oh!" Frank interrupted. "It's a doctor. Doctor something . . . I couldn't hear. Would you two be quiet?"

"A doctor? Must be from Dad's work, right? Someone from the hospital?" Eugene asked.

As Frank was about to answer, the door bumped against his ear as someone tried to push it open. The boys scattered.

"Kids," Dad said, shaking his head. "Time to get ready for dinner. We're having company."

A strange visitor

CHAPTER 2

The first things Jon noticed when the stranger entered their home were the shiny round top of the man's bowler hat and the spark of a match as he lit the pipe pressed between his thin lips. The man wiggled the droplets of heavy rain off his coat, then raised his head to survey them all with a smile.

"Dr. Harrison, it's so good to see you again!" Mom exclaimed.

"Oh, my darling Cecelia!" The man squeezed her into a hug. Their father barely caught the man's jacket as it flew off his shoulders, revealing a tweed suit jacket and striped blue tie underneath. "It has been too long."

"Um . . . could you put that out?" Dad pointed to Dr. Harrison's pipe, and the older man scrambled to snuff it. Jon's nose wrinkled; it smelled awful.

"My apologies, Harvey. Sometimes I forget I'm even using it." The man pulled off his hat, exposing his gray and meager head of hair, and bowed as Aunt Gladys entered the room. "Gladys, you are as lovely as last time I—"

"Don't you sweet-talk me." She poked a finger into the man's chest. "It's good to see you, Anthony. Can I take your bag?"

Jon hadn't even noticed the weather-aged leather doctor's bag the man had dropped by his feet when he'd come in the door. As he handed it to their aunt, it shifted from a mysterious weight.

"I'm happy you were able to make it," Mom said.

"Me too, my dear Cece. I told you I'd call when I was in the area again." The man's wrinkles squished around his eyes as he smiled. "Oh, Gladys, what is that magnificent smell?"

"Lasagna. And it'll get cold if no one eats it. Come on, kids."

Jon was ushered to the dining room table, where Dr. Harrison pulled a chair out first for their mother and then for their aunt before seating himself at the head. Jon's father was helping Clara into the chair next to him; she always liked to climb in sideways, making the chair tilt.

"He looks funny . . ." Jon whispered to Peter.

"Yeah, sounds funny," Frank commented, "like he came from Harry Potter or something?"

"I think you mean he looks and sounds English," Peter corrected. "I think he sounds cool."

Eugene was uncharacteristically quiet and staring at his plate. Why wasn't he glaring at them for their inappropriate whispering?

"Oh, Cecelia, finally I'm meeting the whole family. All your darling children and your . . ." Dr. Harrison gestured at Jon's father but seemed unable to find the right word.

"Husband?" their father offered.

"Of course." Dr. Harrison fidgeted in his seat. "You sure keep yourselves busy with five children, oh my . . ."

"We're happy you could come on such short notice." Mom smiled and served the man a slice of lasagna.

Dr. Harrison rubbed his hands together, licking his lips in anticipation. "Oh, Gladys, that does smell good indeed. I haven't eaten anything since the plane."

"So not from Dad's work?" Jon whispered.

Frank nodded his agreement. "Sounds like he knows Mom and Aunt Gladys well. Maybe a friend of theirs?"

Aunt Gladys cleared her throat—a signal to hush.

"Now, let me see if I get this right. Ernest is your oldest . . ."

"It's actually Eugene," Dad interjected.

"Oh yes, Eugene! How could I have forgotten? Sorry there, my boy. Let's see now, there are the twins and, um . . .

and this little fellow! Then the darling Clara." Dr. Harrison winked at Clara, and she shrunk a little into her seat. Clara was shy, and Jon didn't like that Dr. Harrison made her uncomfortable. "Well, I'm so excited to meet you all."

∩∣∩

Frank hated when they had company over for dinner. The crazy antics that normally happened at the table were unacceptable; instead they were forced to sit and listen to their parents and aunt talk about boring stuff. Frank wished his parents would let them leave the table right after they finished their food, but it was expected they spend at least some time with their dinner guests.

But this visitor was different—mysterious and interesting.

"Doesn't look like he's from Mom's work," Jon whispered while they sat with empty plates. Frank's mom was a police detective for the Naples Florida Police Department. Dr. Harrison was the furthest thing from a police officer.

"Maybe he knows Aunt Gladys?" Frank began, but then Eugene shifted in his chair, distracting him. "Hey, Jon, did you notice Eugene isn't eating?"

"What do I care?" Jon said, but he glanced over at their older brother. Eugene was picking at his food. He hadn't eaten even a mouthful of the generous serving of lasagna Aunt Gladys had given him. Eugene was not known for having a small appetite.

"Well, that was delicious, but I better get to work now," Dr. Harrison said. "My darling Gladys, where did you set my bag?"

"Your bag?" Dad asked.

"Why, yes!" Dr. Harrison looked from their dad's shocked expression to their mom's. "I assumed I would be testing the boys tonight. That is why I'm here. Am I wrong, Cecelia?"

"Well—"

"Perhaps I got their ages wrong. Your boys are ten, right?" Dr. Harrison wiped his face with his napkin and placed it on his plate.

"They are, but—" Frank's mother didn't get the chance to finish before Dr. Harrison crossed his arms, a stern glare on his face.

"They should have come to me for their nine and half year checkup, as Eugene did. These two are overdue. Children their age must have the proper—"

"Yes, but—" Dad's voice had risen to match Dr. Harrison's. The conversation had Frank and Jon sitting on the edge of their seats. This strange visitor was talking about *them*.

"Oh, let me guess, Harvey, you thought if Eugene didn't have the gift, your other children wouldn't either?" The doctor's jaw clenched. "I try to warn parents—"

"Children, you are excused!" Mom cut him off, rising from her chair. The abrupt action took Frank so off guard he stood too. "Gladys, would you take them upstairs to play?"

Before Frank could find out what was going on, their aunt had scooted them from the dining room and shooed them up the staircase to their bedroom. Usually Frank would have loved to be excused early, but not this time. What did his parents not want them to know?

As soon as Aunt Gladys closed the door, Jon turned to Eugene and crossed his arms. "All right, what's going on?"

Eugene's eyes got wide and his nostrils flared.

"Don't pretend you don't know something. Dr. Harrison named you."

"Okay!" Eugene whispered and plopped onto Peter's bed. Peter sat on the floor and handed Clara one of Jon's spaceman action figures to play with.

Eugene sighed. "Yeah, I've met him before."

"When you were nine and a half?" Peter asked. Eugene nodded.

"So, he's a real doctor?" Jon prodded. "Like Dad?"

"I don't think so. No. Maybe."

"Well, he has to be a doctor of something."

"Mom told me he was . . . a doctor of the mind."

Frank cocked his head. The only doctors of the mind he could think of were psychiatrists.

"Like a shrink?" Jon asked, and Eugene shook his head.

"No. I'm not supposed to tell you guys. Dad said I couldn't. He said you weren't old enough."

"Well, we're old enough now." Frank gave a sarcastic snort.

"Did you take a test? What is it for? Does it hurt?" Jon continued to probe excitedly, but their older brother just chewed on his lower lip. Frank knew Eugene always wanted to follow the rules. He hated to do anything that might upset their parents.

"It's a test to see if you have a gift," Eugene finally said. "'A gift in your mind' is what Dad told me. But Dr. Harrison said I don't have one. A gift, I mean. I have a mind." Eugene pointed to his head. "The test didn't hurt me at all, but I have no 'gift,' so I don't know if that changes anything."

"Gift? What does that mean?" Peter asked.

"I don't know. They never told me."

A knock at the bedroom door made Eugene jump.

"Kids?" It was Dad. "Dr. Harrison is leaving. Please come down and say goodbye."

Confused, Frank followed the rest of his siblings down the stairs. At the front door, Dr. Harrison was putting on his coat, and Aunt Gladys was handing him his doctor bag.

"Don't say I didn't warn you, Cecelia." Dr. Harrison swiped the bowler hat out of Mom's hand.

"Goodbye, Dr. Harrison," Peter said, and the other siblings murmured a goodbye as well.

Dr. Harrison paused and walked over to Frank and Jon, staring each of them in the eyes.

"Hmm . . . if you two experience anything extraordinary, give me a call."

With a smirk, Dr. Harrison pulled out a business card and held it out to Frank. As he reached for it, Dr. Harrison grabbed his wrist and flipped his hand over, placing the card in his palm. He acted as if they were simply shaking hands, but Dr. Harrison's curious stare made Frank shrink back.

"Hmm . . . interesting," Dr. Harrison murmured and peered over his shoulder at the other siblings, tilting his hat. Before heading out the door, he kissed their mother on the cheek. "Until another time, my dear. I am sure we will see each other again . . . very soon."

He swished through the door and into the rain, lighting his pipe as he went. Frank turned over the card in his hand and read it.

DR. ANTHONY HARRISON
SERVING THE PERCEPTUALLY GIFTED SINCE 1978

Hearing Things

CHAPTER 3

Jonathon couldn't stop dwelling on Dr. Harrison's strange visit, but whenever he tried to probe his parents for information, he received less than satisfying results. His mother would shake her head, assuring him it was nothing to worry about, while his father stuttered out vague nonresponses. Even Eugene had clammed up on the subject, although he was as clueless as Jon.

Jon was not alone though. Frank and Peter also enjoyed speculating about the doctor's intentions.

"What if they were testing Eugene for mutations, like in X-Men?" Frank suggested one night in their room, tossing a tennis ball at the ceiling from the top bunk. "What if he was supposed to have, like, three arms?"

"Well, we always thought he was from another planet."

Jon laughed from below him, tracing the constellations on the star chart he'd pinned to the bottom of Frank's mattress. From the time he was Peter's age, Jon had fallen to sleep by counting the constellations on his star charts, imagining he was surrounded by millions and millions of stars, traveling through space at light speed, ready to visit any one.

Frank's upside-down head popped over the edge, startling him. "I still do. He sure isn't like the rest of us."

Peter was turning Dr. Harrison's card over in his hands. "Maybe 'perceptually gifted' means you can sense things, like what time it is even if you live in a box, all by yourself, alone, with no windows."

Jon snorted. "What? No! That would be a stupid gift. What would you do all day? Fix watches?"

"I think it would be useful," Peter mumbled.

The conversation died down as, one by one, the boys gradually drifted off to asleep.

Jon's dreams had always felt real to him. This time he was in a marshy field. As he walked, his boots sank into the soil, and the squishy ground sucked at his feet, making him struggle with each step.

"Jon!" a voice called.

Looking down into a murky puddle, Jon spotted his own reflection, but it was different, faceless.

He kicked the water and lifted his head, trying to get a

better sense of his surroundings. Marsh grass extended for hundreds of feet. At the horizon, a line of tall trees was swinging back and forth—which made sense to Jon in the dream. Of course trees moved; they were alive. Their blurry images continued to sway left and right as they marched closer and closer.

"Jon, behind you!" Frank's voice called out.

A vicelike grip closed around Jon's neck, choking him. He reached back to yank whatever it was away, but his hands closed around empty air. Panic shot through his chest as his lungs cried out for oxygen. He fell to his knees and sank into the watery mud, his vision darkening.

He could just make out the dark tree figures hunching over him.

"Help . . ." he whispered, and the grip around his throat tightened. "I'm dying."

A flash of light enveloped him, and he sucked in a giant breath as his eyelids flew open. He was back in his bunk, staring at the star charts, his blanket a tangled mess around his body.

Was I holding my breath in my sleep?

Jon's hand dashed to his neck, and he jumped out of bed to look at himself in the mirror. There was no bruising, no redness; everything was normal. The only other sound in the room was Peter's light snores.

Jon climbed back into his bunk and tried to go back to sleep.

∩∩

Frank could tell at breakfast that something was bothering his twin brother. Jon's normal morning behavior was noisy and disruptive—often a mix of teasing Peter and trying to annoy Eugene. Today, though, Jon silently stared into space, barely touching his food.

Frank could usually read his brother so well it was as if he could hear his thoughts. But this morning, he couldn't seem to get a fix on him; it was frustrating. After trying to begin a conversation twice, Frank snapped his fingers in front of his twin's face.

Jon jumped in his chair. "What?"

"Earth to Jon. Where have you been?" Frank spooned a pile of cereal into his mouth.

"I didn't sleep well," Jon murmured.

"Well, it's time to wake up. The bus will be here soon."

Jon grunted and distractedly cleared his dishes.

Things got even weirder at school. As Frank and Jon headed toward their classroom, the halls seemed louder than usual. It was as if Frank could hear whispering above the regular chatter—voices he couldn't place, conversations that seemed to have no owner.

At his desk in Mr. Hillard's classroom, Frank stuffed his

backpack under his chair. At least the noise level was better within the classroom walls.

While Mr. Hillard wrote math problems on the board, Jon pulled out his pencil and paper from his backpack. "*I hate math . . .*"

"Me too," Frank murmured in agreement.

Jon shot him a confused glance. "You too what?"

"I hate math." Frank quirked an eyebrow as Jon grimaced at him. "You said you hated math, and I agreed."

"Frank, I didn't say anything . . ."

Jon opened his notebook, and Frank sighed. "Sure you didn't . . ." He was certain he'd heard Jon say something, clear as day. But it wasn't unusual for Jon to mess with him.

Mr. Hillard finished writing on the board. "*I'd better start class . . .*" He turned around and scanned the group of students. "*Where is that boy Joe Fletcher again?*"

Frank had to blink twice.

He could have sworn Mr. Hillard had spoken—in fact, he'd heard the words as if they'd been whispered right next to him—but the teacher's mouth hadn't moved. Shaking his head, Frank told himself he was imagining it.

It was a test day, but Frank found it difficult to concentrate. He could hear his brother murmuring answers—and it wasn't just Jon; the rest of the students were also counting, adding, and subtracting aloud. A mush of words and numbers filled the room.

Why isn't Mr. Hillard stopping them?

Frank knew he wasn't supposed to, but he lifted his head to see which of his classmates were making so much noise. With a jolt, he realized no one was speaking.

"Frank, eyes on your own paper," Mr. Hillard's voice, louder than the rest, warned him.

Nodding, Frank glued his eyes to his test again. He had finished just two questions; there were six left and only ten minutes to complete them. In a desperate move to focus on his test, he covered an ear.

The noise didn't get quieter.

He set his pencil down and put both hands over his ears. Maybe he could at least read the question.

Nothing was working. The noise was just as loud as before, and Frank was beginning to sweat. He felt as if he'd read the math problem a hundred times, but he still couldn't comprehend it.

"Franklin? Are you OK?" Mr. Hillard asked. At least, he thought it was Mr. Hillard; there were so many voices in his head he couldn't tell which ones were which anymore.

Unable to form words, Frank just shook his head no.

"All right. You have permission to go to the nurse. We'll figure out your test later, OK?"

Nodding, Frank stood, his hands still on his ears. As he

rushed out the door and into the hall, Frank caught a glimpse of Jon's worried face.

What is happening to me?

Things were quieter in the nurse's office, and Frank was able to relax a bit. Words and whispers still buzzed far away, but he couldn't bring himself to explain to the nurse that he was hearing *voices*.

The nurse wasted no time in getting his mother on the phone. "Mrs. Reed . . . yeah, he's complaining about ringing in his ears. It could be an infection, but I'm not sure. I can't see anything. You should probably take him to see a doctor."

A half hour later, Frank let out a sigh of relief when his mother rushed into the room, her badge displayed on her belt. Her eyes found him in an instant. "There's my boy."

Frank stood up and hugged her. He couldn't wait to go home.

His mother squeezed him tight, then gently held him out at arm's length to get a good look at his face, keeping her hands on his shoulders. "Let's get you out of here," she said, as if sensing his feelings. Without any argument from the staff, she briskly walked him off the school property.

∾↷

After Frank's incident at school, Jon kept a close eye on his brother. By the next morning, Frank was mostly back to normal, if a bit embarrassed by what had happened.

Jon poked him in the shoulder as they ate breakfast. "Carver and Elena asked about you at lunch."

"Gosh"—Frank's face crunched in frustration—"they must think I tried to bail on the math test."

"They know you better than that. You'd never bail." Jon paused. "You're not me, right?"

Frank rolled his eyes at that, and Jon put his hands up defensively. "Sorry."

"It's OK," Frank said with a sigh as they grabbed their backpacks and headed to school.

Even though their teacher gave them more homework than usual, it turned out to be a pretty good Friday. Jon successfully traded the ham-and-cheese sandwich Aunt Gladys had made him for a slice of cold pizza, and his apple for a brownie.

On the bus home, Frank argued with Carver about whether spiders peed. Jon couldn't help but chime in with his own thoughts—he was solidly in the *yes* camp.

Elena, tired of the discussion and the only one with a smartphone, was able to research it online for them. "They waste uric acid, which is near solid and doesn't dissolve in water."

"Eww…" Frank laughed. "What else does it say?"

Fascinated by the article Elena had found, the group

spent the rest of the bus ride and the walk to the Reed's house debating the details.

Heading straight to the backyard, Jon pulled the soccer ball from the basket by the back door and dribbled it around the grass.

"OK, Elena and Frank against me and Jon," Carver yelled. Elena pulled her hair back into a ponytail and gave Frank a high five. Smirking, Jon passed the ball to his friend. Carver soon scored between the two mango trees on the back fence.

"Easy shot." Frank kicked the ball off to Elena, who dribbled it around Carver.

Jon came up on the left side and stole the ball with a swipe of his foot. Even though the grass was dry and crunchy, he could still maneuver the ball easily; however, Elena snuck around to his right and took the ball back.

"Hey!" Jon laughed, and Carver ran after her.

As Jon moved to open space for a pass, a wave of dizziness stopped him in his tracks. His vision blurred, and instead of seeing one Elena dribbling near the mango trees, he saw two. One appeared like a shadow, dribbling ahead while the physical Elena followed it. The shadow figure kicked the shadow ball toward the goal, but it flew too high, sailing over the fence and into neighbor's yard.

The shadows vanished.

The real Elena prepared to kick, and Jon yelled, "Don't!"

Elena turned to him just as her foot made contact with the ball. Due to her broken concentration, it flew too high and landed over the fence.

"Jon!" Frank shouted. "Why'd you do that?"

"What'd you mean?"

"You yelled at me right before I kicked." Elena sneered at him. "Now we have to see if Mr. Ramirez is home to get it back."

"Sorry, I was trying to stop you from kicking—" Jon stopped. His yelling was what had *caused* her to kick it over the fence—saying he was trying to *prevent* her from kicking it over the fence would sound weird. If he told them he had seen Elena's shadow kick the ball over the fence before it happened, they wouldn't believe him.

"Forget it," Elena said and left with Frank and Carver to retrieve the ball.

Jon didn't follow right away; he replayed what had happened in his head and laughed. The sun must have been playing tricks on his eyes. "It's nothing," he told himself and took off to Mr. Ramirez's house.

The Gifted

CHAPTER 4

Jon's feet were trapped in the marshy ground. Even though Frank waved at him to follow, he couldn't move. The trees swayed on the horizon—they were coming, closer and closer. Frank yelled frantically for him to hurry, but Jon continued to sink . . .

"Jon!" A hand grabbed his shoulder and started shaking him. "Jon!"

Sucking in a deep breath, Jon startled awake, his pajamas clinging to his clammy skin. Two little eyes were staring at him. "Peter?"

"You were being loud."

Jon rubbed his eyes, reaching for Peter's shoulder. "Sorry, Pete. I had a weird dream." He raised himself up on his elbows. The sounds of movement and murmuring drifted down from the bunk above. "Is Frank OK?"

"He's been loud too." Peter sighed, crossing his arms over the R2-D2 image on his pajama shirt. "What does a guy have to do to get some sleep around here?"

"Pete, look . . ." As Jon slipped off his bunk, the room tipped, and he grabbed the edge of his bunk frame to steady himself. It was happening again. A shadow figure of Frank appeared, holding its ears and yelling. Ghostly images of his parents rushed into the room to wake his brother, who seemed imprisoned in his own little world. Then, once again, the shadows disappeared. "I think Frank's going to get worse . . ."

"Why do you say that?"

In that moment, Frank's moaning turned into loud crying. Jon rushed up the ladder to the top bunk. Frank was sweating; his body slammed against the bunk bed's barrier as he tossed and turned.

"Stop! I don't want to listen anymore! Stop!" Frank yelled. Rushing footsteps sounded up the stairs, and the bedroom door crashed open. Jon wasn't surprised to see his parents; he knew they would come.

"Franklin?" Dad said.

Jon jumped from the bunk. His father lifted Frank from his bed and laid him on Peter's, smoothing Frank's red hair from his face and whispering to calm him.

"Stop talking!" Frank yelled, still asleep. "I don't want to listen. Be quiet!"

Putting a hand to Frank's head, his dad shot their mom a worried look. "He's not running a fever, Cecelia. Franklin? Hey, buddy." Rubbing his son's shoulders and patting his cheek did nothing to wake Frank.

Mom sat on the edge of the bed and pulled Frank into her arms. Her hand slipped to his chest, over his heart. "Shh, baby . . . it's OK. Focus on my voice. My voice only. Shh . . ." Frank kept murmuring quietly. "Listen, Frank. Listen to my voice only." Gradually, Frank relaxed in her arms.

"Why isn't he waking up, Mom?" Peter asked. Their parents glanced at each other, and Dad sighed.

"Harvey, I think it's time we call Dr. Harrison," Mom said, and he nodded.

"I'll take care of it. Come on, you two. Frank is safe with Mom." He scooted them out to the couches in the living room.

As soon as their dad had left the room, Peter rounded on Jon. "Dr. Harrison! What do you think this means? Is Frank going to be OK?"

"I don't know."

"Well, you must know something. How did you know Frank was going to get worse?"

Jon rubbed his neck. How *had* he known? It was so

confusing—all of it.

A groggy Eugene appeared on the stairs and raised his eyebrows when he saw his brothers. "What's going on?"

"That's what we'd like to know." Peter crossed his arms. Pushing his glasses up the bridge of his nose, Peter flopped back against the couch.

They'd been sitting in the living room for almost an hour when Dad finally came down and led them back to bed. Frank's bunk was empty, but Dad assured him Frank was sound asleep in his parents' room and would be fine.

Jon tried to believe his dad, but he couldn't help feeling betrayed. He didn't like being left in the dark. What was happening to Frank? What was happening to them? Before he closed his eyes, he snuck a small card from under Frank's pillow and flipped it over and over in his hand—the business card for an older man with a bowler hat and pipe. Perhaps Dr. Harrison would have some answers.

∽⌒

The previous night had left Frank exhausted. Thankfully, the voices in his head had quieted, and Mom let him rest during the day on the couch in the living room. Jon came to sit with him after breakfast, and they played some video games. Whenever Frank felt an episode of voices coming, he would call Mom, and she would sit with him to calm his panic.

"Don't worry Frank," Jon encouraged him. "Mom says Dr. Harrison will be here tonight."

"OK." Frank didn't want to admit it to Jon, but he was scared. "Will you stay with me?"

"Of course." Jon smiled.

By the time Dr. Harrison arrived, the voices in Frank's head had once again become louder and more chaotic. He shut his eyes tight, struggling to follow any conversation. *I'm losing my mind*, he thought. *Dr. Harrison is going to take me away.*

As if sensing his fears, his mother reached out and stroked his face, and a small wave of peace swept over him.

Dr. Harrison pulled a chair up beside the couch.

"I have something" was all Frank could decipher of Dr. Harrison's words. He opened his eyes to see the older man digging through his doctor bag to retrieve a stone on a long chain.

The doctor leaned forward to drape the chain around Frank's neck. As soon as the stone touched his chest, all the random voices and noise were sucked out of the air. The only sounds he heard were people shuffling in front of him and a gasp from Jon.

"There we go." Dr. Harrison smiled. "Now, tell me, Franklin, does that feel better?"

"I feel . . . I feel normal." Frank sat up and clutched the stone. "What is this?" He rubbed its smooth surface between his fingers, studying it closely. It wasn't jewelry. It was a heavy pebble, dark purple, with fiery swirls of blue inside.

"That, my boy, is a stardust stone," Dr. Harrison said. "It will inhibit some of your abilities until I have completed my examination." All Frank could do was nod, confused but relieved to have silence in his head. "Cecelia, this is a good sign. Obviously, the stone assisted, which I expected based on my theory."

"So, you can help him?" Dad asked.

Dr. Harrison glared at him. "Of course I can help him." He shuffled around in his bag again, mumbling under his breath, "This could have been avoided if I had been allowed to examine the boys."

Frank's eyes widened as Dr. Harrison pulled out a strange device made of rubber tubing and metal. Straightening his back with a grumble, the man put the tool around his neck. It looked like a stethoscope, except the ear portion resembled headphones, and the part that was usually placed over the heart was divided into two pieces instead of one.

"What is that? A stethoscope?"

"Oh, this? Something like that. This is a preceptoscope. This isn't made for listening to the heart. It listens to the *mind.*" Dr. Harrison cleared his throat and took out a notepad and pen from his inner jacket pocket. "All right, Franklin, tell me about your symptoms. Your mother says you're hearing voices."

Franklin bit his lip. Hearing Dr. Harrison say it out loud made Frank feel even crazier.

As if sensing his unease, Dr. Harrison put his hands up. "Oh no, my boy, you are not losing your mind." He smiled. "In fact, today we will discover amazing things about your mind. Please tell me what has been happening."

Sighing, Frank describe the sensation of being surrounded by people who were talking to him all at once, but no one was there, or if there were people, no one was speaking. "I could even hear voices over people talking to me, but no one else hears them. I can't sleep, I can't focus, I'm anxious all the time."

Dr. Harrison nodded, murmuring and writing notes. When Frank had finished, the doctor pulled the preceptoscope up, breathed on the ends, and rubbed them together. "You mind if I take a listen?"

Dr. Harrison placed the earphones over his head but not on his ears. To Frank's surprise, he placed the end pieces on either side of Frank's head and pressed them firmly. Jon held back a giggle at the sight.

Frank's thoughts were interrupted by something else—a voice. "*Ah, yes, how delightful! Franklin, you can hear me, can't you?*" It was Dr. Harrison, but the man had not spoken out loud. The doctor smirked at Frank and lifted his eyebrow.

"Yes," Frank said, and Dr. Harrison removed the preceptoscope from his head.

"An easy diagnosis, my dear Cece!" The man grinned from ear to ear.

"What's wrong with me?"

"Wrong? Oh, no, my boy, there is nothing wrong with you at all. In fact, you are healthy as a horse! You are unique, gifted, specially abled. Like your mother and myself."

"Mom?" both the boys said at once, looking at her.

Her cheeks tinged with a light blush. "It's true."

"But what does it mean?" Jon asked. "Gifted?"

Dr. Harrison once again glared at their father. "In many cases, parents prepare their children for this time. However, there are *those*"—he grunted—"who hide this knowledge from their family. Especially when they are afraid of it."

"Now, wait a minute—" Dad took a step toward Dr. Harrison.

"Harvey." Mom's voice stopped him. "Let me handle this."

"Cece, allow me—" Dr. Harrison said, but didn't finish. Frank's Mom had given him the eyes. "Of course, it is your right to tell them."

"I learned about my gift when I was a little girl. When I found out, it was like you, Frank. No one had ever told me about gifted people." Mom moved to sit by Frank's feet.

"The last person in my family who was gifted lived several generations before me. I was scared." She paused, a sad smile on her face. "I felt so much all the time. I was lucky Aunt Gladys was resourceful. She found Dr. Harrison, and he took care of me. Helped me learn about my gift and how to use it properly."

Dr. Harrison sat back in his chair, his stare glued to his shoes. Frank was sure there was more to his mother's story. "I was ten years old. It is typical, in a family of gifted individuals, to have their children examined at ten to determine what gift they have. Sometimes though . . ." She paused and glanced at Dad.

"Sometimes, when you are married to someone who is not gifted . . ." Dad added for her with a smile.

"You, Dad?" Frank asked, and Dad smirked.

"Yes. I'm not gifted, at least not in the way you and Mom are. And when one parent is not perceptually gifted, the gene may not be passed down to their children. Your mother's family did not always have gifted relatives either. Her father and her grandfather were not gifted."

"It can make things hard to predict," Mom said. "In fact, we took Eugene to Dr. Harrison when he was nine and a half. His results were negative."

"So, we assumed—"

"A poor assumption," Dr. Harrison interjected, huffing

his frustrations through his nose, "and here we are. You, Franklin, have been given a gift. The gift of telepathy!"

"Telepathy?" Frank's eyes widened, and a shiver ran down his back.

"Yes, my boy. You will be able to hone the skill and art of reading minds." Dr. Harrison grinned. "I am a telepath by gift as well."

"Mom too?"

"No, your mother's gift is empathy. She can sense and manipulate feelings."

"Whoa!" both the boys said together, making everyone laugh.

∩∩

Telepath. Empath. What other abilities were out there? Could there be a gift for shadow figures and headaches?

"Jon?"

Jon had been so lost in thought that he jumped when he heard his mother calling his name.

"Hmmm . . ." Dr. Harrison was staring at him. "Jonathan, right?"

"Doctor?" Mom asked.

"My dear, I think there is something your son is not telling you." Jon's eyes widened as the man stared at him. "You wonder how I know? I can read minds, Jonathan, remember? May I, Cecelia?"

"Of course." Mom touched Jon's shoulder to reassure him.

The older man turned his chair to face Jon. Peering into his eyes, Dr. Harrison took out his notepad, as he had for Frank. "All right now, let's see . . ."

Jon squirmed in his chair, momentarily distracted by his aunt coming into the room with a tray of tea.

"Stay, Aunt Gladys," Mom said, and Aunt Gladys scooted Frank over to take a seat next to him on the couch.

"Are you hearing voices, Jonathan?" Dr. Harrison asked, licking his fingers to turn pages in his notes.

"No, yes, maybe . . ." Jon replied.

Dr. Harrison raised an eyebrow and wrote something down. "How about feeling unusual waves of emotions such as anger, sadness, or excitement, especially in a group of people or family?"

"No."

"Do you find things are moving without you touching them, or uncontrolled items are being flung through space when you are present?"

"Um, no." Jon was confused by these questions—none of these were even close to what he was experiencing.

"Do you find yourself able to remember everything you see and read, and are you constantly reviewing it in your waking or sleeping state?"

"No."

"Hmmm . . ." Dr. Harrison grunted and wrote some more notes. "Have you felt differently when touching objects or people, where you may pick up on ideas or memories?"

"I don't think so . . ." Jon watched as the doctor shook his head and jotted something else down.

"Perhaps I was wrong . . ." Dr. Harrison sighed.

"Wait," Jon said. This was his moment to get answers. "What if I'm seeing things before they happen?"

Aunt Gladys gasped.

Dr. Harrison dug into his bag for another book and began flipping through the pages. "Well, Jonathan, that is another thing entirely, though I am less familiar with it. Let me see . . ." Dr. Harrison put on the preceptoscope, pressing the small metal plates against Jon's head. For several moments, nothing happened, then Jon felt another swell of dizziness. His eyes rolled back in his head, and his body went slack in the chair.

From a black mist, a memory rolled in of Frank falling onto the patio table, a soccer ball flying over a fence, and then a heavy weight pressing on his chest. His dreams were being pulled to the surface of his mind. The grassy field, the muddy bog, the hands around his neck.

Jon cried out.

"Stop! Stop, you're hurting him," Mom yelled.

Jon's eyes flew open to see the dumbstruck doctor, breathing in heavy gasps, the preceptoscope still clutched in his hand inches from Jon's head.

A hand touched Jon's cheek. He turned to meet his mother's worried eyes.

"You OK, Jonny?" she whispered.

"Of course," Jon said, though he felt far from it. He gave her a smile and a wink to ease her fears.

Dr. Harrison cleared his throat. "Impossible," he murmured, but smiled at them. "Both your boys are gifted. Jonathan's is . . . particularly interesting. I haven't seen a case like his before, but I do know someone who has. I will need to make a few phone calls before they go to West Hills."

"West Hills?" Frank asked.

"It's a school," Mom said.

"A school for the gifted," Dr. Harrison added as he packed his bag.

"Wait!" Jon said. "We have to go to a different school?"

"Yes," Mom said with a sad smile. "I went there too. Aunt Gladys had to send me there."

"I didn't have the skills to teach her how to use her gift." Aunt Gladys's wrinkled eyes smiled, but her voice quivered a little.

"Where is it?"

"It's in another state."

"You are required to live on campus there," the doctor said as he stood up and put his bowler hat on. He whispered to their parents, "I will inform the school of their immediate enrollment. Term has already started, but they will find room. Late admission isn't unheard of."

"Dr. Harrison," Dad said, "are you saying they *have* to go?"

"Cecelia, help me out here." The doctor huffed in exasperation. "They must. It is our law, it is our way." Dr. Harrison turned a stern face to the whole family. "Besides, I am mandated to share their names and gifts with the society once they have been confirmed. Cece, I told you the whole truth, and you understood it perfectly." He bent down to speak to the twins. "Boys, inappropriate use of these gifts can be a danger not only to yourself but to those around you. That is why it is important for you to attend school, and . . . it is required."

Squeezing past Jon's dad, Dr. Harrison leaned in to give Mom a kiss on the cheek in a warm gesture before turning to a teary-eyed Aunt Gladys. "I promise to take care of them."

"You better, Anthony." The warning in her voice was clear.

"Sir, your stone?" Frank was taking off the necklace, but the doctor stopped him.

"It's yours now. Return it to me when you no longer need it. It's time for me to go. And don't worry, Harvey . . . Yes, don't give me that look. I can read your mind. They will be in the best of care. I'll let myself out." After bowing to them all, he turned to leave, but Jonathan stopped him.

"Sir, wait, you never told me. What is my gift?"

"Forgive me." He gave Jon a genuine smile, a twinkle in his eye. "You can tell the future, Jonathan. At least, you will be able to someday. A very rare gift indeed. Excuse me." Dr. Harrison slipped out the door and shut it securely behind him.

Trick or Treat

CHAPTER 5

"Why are you changing schools, again?" Carver asked during lunch.

"We're going to my mom's school." Frank took a bite of his sandwich. He couldn't tell Carver the real reason; his parents had said it was a secret. And besides, would his friend even believe him? He could hardly accept it himself. "Mom says it's a good school."

"Yeah, it's one of those schools where you eat, sleep, and don't go home," Jon piped in, momentarily distracted from his bargaining with Elena. "My PB and J for the tuna . . . I'll even throw in the fruit snack?"

"Like a boarding school? And it's in Washington DC?" Elena shook her head at Jon and bit into her sandwich. "Negotiations are closed."

Jon smirked back. "I'd still eat it."

"You'd eat anything, Jon." Frank rolled his eyes. "No, not DC. Washington State."

"I have an uncle in Washington," said Carver. "My dad says he visits us here to get away from the rain. It rains every day there."

"Carver, it rains every day here." Jon chuckled. "Especially during hurricane season."

"Well, good news for you. They don't have hurricanes in Washington." Elena grinned and settled in to eat her tuna sandwich, her elbows on the table.

"No hurricanes? Awesome!" Jon flicked a potato chip at her.

"Jon!" She shoved her chair back. "Don't start a food fight. Last time we got detention for a week."

"I heard they have earthquakes instead." Carver shivered. Frank almost choked on his lunch. "What?"

"Yeah, they have volcanoes too . . . active ones!"

"Volcanoes. Well, I'm screwed . . . Frank, we need to practice more hot lava. I'm not dying because you can't hold on to me."

His brother winked at him, but Frank turned red. It was no secret he wasn't all that athletic, particularly compared to Jon.

"Carver, stop it!" Elena punched him lightly in the

shoulder. "Listen, boys, when was the last time you heard on the news about an earthquake or volcano eruption in Washington? Like, never!"

She glanced at Frank, which made him blush even more. As much as he wished otherwise, he wasn't brave like his brother, and Elena knew it. He was scared of change, and this was going to be a big one.

"Sorry," Carver whispered. "It's just that I'm going to miss you both." The table got quiet. Even Jon was unusually silent.

Elena sighed. "Me too. It won't be the same here without you."

They'd eaten lunch with Elena and Carver almost every day since first grade. They were their squad, their team, and now things would be . . . different.

"Hey . . ." Jon finally spoke up. "I have a whoopee cushion in my backpack. Frank, whaddaya say we give Mr. Hillard a Reed brothers' farewell? What's the worst that could happen? We get detention?"

"God help Washington." Elena gave Jon a high five.

After school, the four friends took the long route by the neighborhood creek to the Reed home. They paused only to skip rocks on the swampy creek water, scaring away a couple of tiny lizards. The sun warmed Frank through his T-shirt. He would miss afternoons like this one, when the humidity was low and you didn't sweat through your clothes.

As they got closer to home, Jon recapped the episode of Mr. Hillard and the whoopee cushion: "He was so red in the face, I thought his mustache was going to catch fire!"

Elena laughed as they climbed the stairs to the twin's bedroom. "I have an idea! Let's trick or treat!"

"It's not Halloween yet." Carver tossed his backpack on the bed.

"Does it matter?" Jon said, and Frank raced to pull out the Halloween costumes. They wouldn't be here for Halloween, so why not wear them now?

Elena borrowed Eugene's bike and Carver took Peter's, and soon they were racing through the neighborhood like birds released from their cages. Jon wore his Darth Vader mask and gloves, while Carver used his Vader cape and chest plate. Elena was wearing Frank's Thor helmet and armor, while Frank wore the cape and carried the hammer.

As they traveled door to door, they held out their hands and said the magic phrase that brought smiles to the neighbors who knew them. Many didn't have candy but scrounged around for snacks, like granola bars and raisins. Mrs. Tadema gave them each five-dollar bills, which they held in the air like trophies as they ran back to the bikes.

Later, Frank realized the neighbors must have known it was his and Jon's last day in the neighborhood.

After their pockets were filled, they headed back, dropping their bikes in the backyard and lying on the grass under the mango tree to count and trade their loot.

Mom came out to check on them. "Wait there . . ."

She came back with her phone to take a picture, and they posed in their best superhero stances.

Frank knew he would remember this day for a long time.

∩⌒

Jonathan scooted into the window seat, excited he didn't have to fight for it. His mother and brother were sitting in the row in front of him and Dad. He watched, face pressed to the window, as people below loaded the plane with luggage.

"How long is the flight, Dad?" Jon started opening and closing the window cover in fascination.

"It's about five and half hours, buddy, and stop that!" Dad reached over and stilled Jon's hand, then leaned back in his seat to close his eyes.

Not only was his father a nervous flyer; he'd been bothered about something for days. A couple nights ago, Jon had stayed up late with his dad to watch the Star Wars movies, but instead of making his dad happy, it just seemed to make him more depressed. Dad had asked Jon to hug him, and even though Jon wasn't one to hug much, he'd hugged his dad hard and sat close to him on the couch until they fell asleep around midnight.

Dad didn't want them to leave. While Jon was excited about the new school and adventures, he was going to miss his family. Mostly Clara and Peter. And, yes, if he admitted it, he would miss Eugene . . . eventually.

Eugene had rolled his eyes at dinner last night. "They'll be back for Christmas in a couple months. I don't know why it's a big deal . . ."

"I don't want them to go." Peter frowned. "They're the only ones who play with me."

"Come on, Pete, all you do is mope around and read books anyway . . ."

"Hey, Genie." Frank said. "Pete is just . . . misunderstood."

"That's right!" Peter did a double take at Frank. "Wait . . ."

"Don't worry, Pete, the greatest of us all are always misunderstood." Jon had winked and ruffled his hair.

It hadn't been easy saying goodbye to them.

When he, Frank, and their parents had left for the airport, Eugene didn't say much, but he side-punched Jon in the shoulder and told him not to get into too much trouble. Peter cried and hung on to Jon's and Frank's necks. Their Aunt Gladys was able to pull him away so the boys could get in the car.

Clara stayed quiet. She hugged them both and then handed them a picture she'd drawn of herself.

"So we can remember you while we're at school?" Jon had asked, and he'd been rewarded with a smile and a nod.

As the plane taxied out, the flight attendants began going over what to do in an emergency, but Jon wasn't listening. His gaze was fixed on the ground, at the rapidly passing runway lines.

"All right, Han, let's engage the hyperdrive . . ." He pulled out his Han Solo action figure and pressed it against the window.

A loud roar filled the air as the plane sped faster and faster and buildings whizzed past. Finally, Jon felt the wheels lift off the ground and the plane's nose tilt upward. For a moment, he worried the plane would scrape the ground, like the back of his skateboard when he tried to do a wheelie, but the plane ascended flawlessly. The ground drifted farther away, and Jon sucked in a breath as his stomach tumbled, as if he were on a roller coaster at the fair.

"Goodbye, Florida," Frank said from the seat in front of him. "We'll be back soon."

The view as the plane pressed higher into the sky was more than Jon could have imagined. "What is that, Dad?" He pointed to the watery green surface below.

Dad peeked over to see. "The Everglades. They stretch for miles. You went there a couple times with school, remember?"

"Yeah." Jon's brows shot up. "I didn't know they were so

big."

New geometric shapes formed on the ground—circles, squares, and grids. "Aliens?"

"No." Dad chuckled. "Farms have large machines that water and harvest the crops. They make circular shapes. The squares and lines are made by properties and roads."

Soon the plane was gliding above big fluffy white clouds. "It's like being in heaven," Jon said in awe.

"It is very beautiful." Dad sat back, closing his eyes again, one hand on his stomach.

The light vibration of the plane relaxed Jon, allowing his thoughts to drift. What if he could jump on the clouds outside? Would it be like a trampoline? Yes, but he would float, like in space, flying through the sky but coming down to brush the next cloud with his tiptoes. If he sat at the cloud's edge, would he be able to see the whole world? Maybe he'd see hikers on the mountaintops or villages in the valleys or even himself from above, standing in a swampy marsh, his boots sinking into the soft earth . . .

"Jon!" a disembodied voice called.

∩∩

"Jonathan, son!" Dad shook the groaning and thrashing boy. Frank peered over his seat to watch.

"Is he OK?" A rather large graying man next to Dad

asked.

"Yes, he just fell asleep. Must be a bad dream. Jon?"

As Dad shook his shoulders slightly, Jon's eyes shot open, and he gasped. "What?"

"You OK?"

"Yeah, I'm OK. I had a bad dream." Jon leaned back into his seat, and Frank turned around again. It wasn't the first time Jon had had a nightmare; he groaned in his sleep almost every other day—sometimes more dramatically—but Jon never complained or talked about it.

Before long, a voice over the speakers announced they were starting their descent. As the plane broke through the layer of clouds, Frank finally caught sight of the ground below, a landscape of huge organic curves dusted with white.

"Dad, what are those?" Frank heard Jon ask.

"Those, buddy, are the Cascade Mountains."

"Wow!" Frank pressed his face to the window as a huge rocky mountain flashed into view, its cap white with snow.

"Mt. Rainer, I believe."

"It's beautiful, boys, isn't it?" Mom joined the observation party. "I never get tired of seeing it."

As the plane grew closer to the runway, it started shaking from turbulence.

"Takeoff was cool, but I bet landing will be awesome!" Jon laughed.

School for the Perceptually Gifted

CHAPTER 6

The landing was awful—bumpy and turbulent. It seemed to Frank as if the plane was going to land on a parking lot full of cars; then, in the blink of an eye, a runway was under them. The loud, disturbing blare eventually quieted as the engines powered down, silencing completely as they taxied to the gate.

At the baggage claim, Frank glimpsed a figure in a shining black bowler hat and gray wool suit scanning the crowd.

"Dr. Harrison"—Mom walked over to the older gentlemen—"this is a surprise."

With a mischievous grin, Dr. Harrison took both of Mom's hands in his. "Yes, yes, but isn't it a magnificent one?" He laughed. "The school board was inquiring as to who would welcome the boys. I, of course, volunteered right away."

"Great," Dad lightly growled.

"Be nice, Harvey." Mom threw him a sharp look. "It's a sweet gesture. It's so good to see you again, Dr. Harrison."

"My dear Cecelia, always a pleasure to see you and your family—and you too, Herman."

Frank and Jon giggled, and Dad gave them a humoring glare.

"Now, we must get your bags. The school sent a van with a driver to take us there."

Outside, Frank shielded his eyes against the sun and the cloudless blue sky. "Isn't it supposed to rain in Washington?" he mumbled, digging in his backpack for sunglasses.

"Why, yes, all the time!" Dr. Harrison said. "Just not today."

Despite the sun, a rush of wind sent a chill through Frank's body, and he rubbed his arms as they prickled with goosebumps. Dad handed him this winter coat, and Frank rushed to pull it on.

"I thought it was October, not January?" Jon shivered. "Why does it feel like forty degrees outside?"

"It's colder here, sweetheart," Mom said. "It's even colder in the winter. You'll get used to it."

Frank's teeth chattered. "I don't think so."

The adults chuckled.

"I'll give you long underwear for Christmas." Dad poked him, and the boys moaned.

"All right"—Dr. Harrison opened the van door—"everyone aboard."

Settling into the large heated van and wrapped in his cozy coat, Frank found it hard to keep his eyes open. After only a few minutes, he'd drifted off.

Eventually a small nudge woke him, and Frank wiped a line of drool from his mouth. How long had he been asleep? It felt like minutes, but a peek at the van's digital clock told him it had been at least a couple hours.

"Frank look." Jon pointed out the window.

Frank rubbed his eyes and squinted. They were traveling down a narrow highway, the landscape on each side unlike anything he had seen before. One side was a jagged wall of rock and vegetation—small bushes and thin trees. A passing sign warned that tumbling rocks would occasionally hit the road, which explained the iron wire net hanging over the more precarious areas.

On the other side were trees—so many trees, some as tall as buildings he'd seen in Miami. They grew in close, dark clusters, allowing sparse light to shine through.

"Evergreen trees," Dr. Harrison whispered to the twins. "They're always green, all year round. They don't lose their leaves."

Mixed within the evergreens were trees with large branches and leaves of gold, red, and orange. They sprinkled their colors onto the road as the wind pushed them back and forth. Frank had seen places like this on TV before, but seeing it in real life was a whole different thing.

As they continued up the mountain, the trees grew closer and closer to the road until their branches touched across it, like a bridge for squirrels to cross over the highway. Sunlight peeked through only occasionally, making rays of light for the van to drive through.

Excited gasps from beside Frank made him turn. Jon was pointing to rivers visible through the trees. Glacier water from the mountaintops birthed white, angry waves that rushed over the rocky landscape. Perhaps they'd get to play in the river—maybe even ride a raft down it!

Soon, they turned onto another less-maintained road of compacted gravel and dirt. The forest was so dense Frank didn't see the marker for the school until they'd pulled right up to it.

There, hanging over two pillars, a sign with faded lettering read, "West Hill School for the Perceptually Gifted."

"Ah, we have arrived, my children!"

Frank and Jon pressed their heads between the front and passenger seats. As the van drove around a corner and descended down a narrow trail shielded by low-hanging branches, a large roundabout driveway became visible. It encased a grassy field with a decent-sized fountain. Beyond that was a massive two-story brick building with a walking porch on both levels. A huge staircase and banisters led from the driveway to the building's front doors.

"Wow, we could put, like, eight of our houses into that building," Jon said in amazement.

Dr. Harrison leaned in. "You could, indeed. The older buildings on this property used to belong to the US Government. The property and several standing buildings were sold to the school decades ago."

Frank squinted. "It doesn't look like a school."

"That's because it wasn't originally meant to be one. We're not quite sure what the government used it for—I assume some special secret training." As soon as the van stopped, Dr. Harrison shuffled over to the door and jumped out, straightening his suit jacket and bowler hat. "Wait here while I go get the superintendent, Professor Mortensen."

He pranced up the stairs and into the school, leaving Frank and Jon to stare at the large building before them, slack-jawed. Behind them, the van driver removed the boys' trunks and tumbled them onto the ground.

"Wow . . ." Dad finally said, "that is some old house. Think of all the hidden places there must be to explore."

"Really?" Jon's ears perked up. "You think so?"

"Well," Mom acknowledged, "I managed to discover some very cool places here."

"Where?" Frank asked.

"I'd be taking the fun away if I didn't let you find them for yourselves." Mom's eyes sparkled, but soon her attention was redirected. Frank followed her gaze to a tall man with a dark complexion approaching them. Mom reached out to shake his hand. "Ah, Professor Mortensen."

"Cece!" Professor Mortensen laughed warmly, running one hand over his thin mustache and beard. "How long have we known each other? Please, it's Richard."

After greeting their parents, the professor turned to the twins. He was wearing a white button-up shirt, slacks, and a navy-blue blazer with a weird crest on it; Frank assumed it was a school logo.

But to you boys, it is Professor Mortensen.

Frank heard the man speak, but his mouth didn't move. Jon gasped, and Frank gripped the stone around his neck, confused. Wasn't the stone supposed to prevent him from hearing thoughts?

"I heard that . . ." Frank said out loud. "Did I read your mind?"

"Oh no, Franklin." Professor Mortensen guessed which twin he was with ease. "I let you hear it. I know you're gifted to read minds. You and I both have this telepathic ability. I also allowed Jonathan to hear." *And now, only you can hear me, young Mr. Reed.*

Frank was taken aback. He looked around, and indeed, no one else seemed to have heard the professor's last sentence.

"How did you know my name?" Jon's eyebrows lifted. "How did you know I wasn't Frank—"

"Jon, he can read minds. Duh!" Frank cut in, fascinated. There were more people like him!

"What did he say to you?" Dad asked.

Jon smirked. "He told us we have to call him Professor Mortensen."

"Harvey, this is Richard Mortensen. We were old classmates here," Mom said. Dad shook the superintendent's hand.

"It's a pleasure to meet you, Dr. Reed."

"Harvey."

"Harvey." Professor Mortensen nodded. "Now, are we all ready for the tour?"

They started climbing the large staircase up to the school. Frank's eyes wandered everywhere, but he didn't see anyone else outside. Maybe all the other kids were in class?

"Our campus stretches out in a several-mile radius from the main building. There are many other buildings, as well as walkways and paths."

Frank almost collided with his brother, who had stopped

on the stairs. Following Jon's line of sight, Frank spotted a large crest over the school door. A golden crying eye lay in the center of six spurs, which surrounded it in a sun-like pattern. Each spur had a dot over it, and two dots appeared to swirl around the eye while two wavy lines shot from its side.

It was the same emblem on Professor Mortensen's jacket.

Jon gaped for several seconds at the golden crest, but soon he realized he was holding up the tour and rushed to catch up to his family.

Inside, he couldn't help but stare at the polished wood floors beneath his feet, ornate molding on the wall, and large staircase adorning the main entry. Whatever the school had been before, it had obviously functioned very differently. Evidence of the building's transformation were everywhere. New walls, probably constructed when the school was established, blended in poorly with the one-hundred-year-old design of older ones.

"This is the main hall, entryway to all staff offices and several classrooms. This area also connects us with the cafeteria and assembly halls. My office is located to the right there. Hopefully, you won't need to visit often."

Jon threw a sly smile at Frank.

As they walked the halls, Jon hardly listened to the

conversation between his father and the professor. In the foyer, high above his head, a large iron chandelier hung, draped with spikes pointing toward the ground. Each light fixture was a little school crest, encased in gold.

It wasn't long before he was lagging again.

Jon skipped back over to the small group as they gathered outside a large wooden door. A rusty bronze keyhole beneath the doorknob reminded Jon once again how old the building was.

Rubbing his hands together, the professor turned to the twins. "This room here is for our sagacity students." In response to their confused stares, he cleared his throat. "I keep forgetting, you two didn't grow up in a traditionally gifted home."

"What he means to say is that you're just learning about this world," Mom corrected and kissed Dad's cheek.

"Yes, thank you, Cece. Sagacity is a special gift. It allows you to gain and retain knowledge with ease and understanding. We can peek in on a lesson."

Professor Mortensen opened the door and quietly ushered their family inside. The classroom looked more like an enormous library. Rows and rows of bookshelves lined every wall.

"Peter would love this," Frank whispered to Jon.

Seated in the middle of the room were about forty kids, from Jon's age to just about high school. They each held a book, flipping pages every few seconds, writing without looking at their papers. In the front, the teacher, a thin young man with dark hair and thick-framed glasses, leaned back behind a larger desk, his feet crossed on top of it. He was wearing a similar navy blazer to Professor Mortensen and held a rather hefty book in his hands.

"That is our sage studies and arithmetic teacher, Professor Wyatt." Mortensen pointed to the man before guiding them back out into the hall.

"What are the kids doing?" Dad asked.

"Our sagacity students have the ability to see words on a page and then repeat or write down what they've read with perfect accuracy. They are being tested on their photogenic memory speed."

The professor took them farther down the hall, pointing out the cafeteria, which was surprisingly normal. It was an add-on to the older building—new in comparison to the rest of the facility.

"Over this way is our gymnasium. We have assembly in here, as well as PE, basketball, volleyball, and dodgeball."

"Do you have soccer?" Jon asked eagerly.

"We have a school league, actually." The superintendent smiled at him, and Jon gave Frank a fist bump. "The other thing our gym is used for is our telekinesis studies."

"Teleken-what?" Frank's eyes got big.

Professor Mortensen laughed and pushed the door to

the gym open. "Why don't you look for yourself? They're practicing now."

"Practicing what?" Jon asked, but his question was answered as they peered into the room. A class of students were twirling stuffed animals in the air and laughing.

One girl was making a teddy bear go through the basketball hoop over and over. Another student was tossing her kitten toy as high as the gym ceiling. Neither one touched their objects, which floated freely through the air. A petite young woman with long dark straight hair was moving from student to student, giving instructions.

"That is Professor Yang, over there," Mortensen said. "She teaches telekinesis studies and physical education."

"Do all your instructors teach multiple studies?" Dad asked.

"Yes. We teach our students how to use and control their gifts, but we also keep them up to the same education level as their peers. All our teachers are required to both be certified in an academic study and have attained master level for the gift they instruct on."

The next stop on the tour was on the second floor, where they entered a lengthy hallway lined with classroom doors. Professor Mortensen guided them into the first classroom, pressing a finger to his lips. Inside were long tables with benches that seated students on each side. They were partnered, staring at each other in complete silence. Every so often a student would giggle or make a goofy face, but then a short balding man would whack the desk near them with his ruler.

Mortensen nodded to the stubby man as he shooed them out into the hall again. "Telepathy studies . . ." he whispered, closing the door behind him. "Professor Owens, well, he can be a little strict, but he is the best. He also teaches the English courses."

Jon glanced over at Frank, unsure what staring at someone's face had to do with telepathy. Thank goodness it was something Frank would have to endure and not him.

Another room farther down the hall was furnished with couches and big puffy chairs. Music was playing on an old record player in the corner, and the students scattered throughout were laughing, crying, and dancing. It looked very disorganized. "Empathy studies. Looks like they're doing a free feelings exercise. They seem to do those a lot."

Mortensen smiled and pointed to a woman with pixie-cut brown hair and a red bandana tied around her head. She was sitting cross-legged, eyes closed, on a yoga mat with a group of three students beside her, whom she was leading in a breathing exercise. "Professor Vidra. She teaches our empathic students and our social studies courses."

The next classroom was clear of desks and instead filled with piles of *stuff*. "It looks like a museum," Jon said to

Frank.

In a clearing in the middle, however, students sat in chairs surrounding a Grecian pedestal. An older lady, with russet-brown skin and silver-streaked black hair braided along her shoulders, was placing an object on the pedestal with care. One by one, each student stood and spoke to the group, but Jon was too far away to hear their conversation.

"What are they doing?" Frank asked.

"They are discussing what they perceive from the object in the middle. These are psychic studies, and that there is Professor Gonzalez. She will also be your science teacher."

As Jon turned to follow the group out the door, his eyes met Gonzalez's for a second or so, and she smiled at him before returning her attention to the class.

"All right," Professor Mortensen said, "our other classrooms are very similar to what you have back home, boys. They are used primarily for our regular academic studies. Shall we tour the grounds?"

They headed back down the stairs.

Jon stopped midway when he realized something. "Sir, I didn't see my classroom or teacher. Where is it?" Perhaps they met outside or in another building?

Something about the professor's hesitation made Jon nervous. Mortensen turned toward him, meeting Jon at eye level since he was still standing several steps up the stairs.

"Mr. Reed, we do not have a classroom dedicated to your gift. In fact, your gift is very rare. The last time this school had prophecy studies was over four decades ago, and there were two students. We are very excited to have you."

Mortensen's eyes wandered to Jon's parents. The slight frown on Mom's face made Jon feel weird, and disappointment started to seep into his gut.

"But don't worry Jonathan." Mortensen placed a hand on his shoulder. "We've made special accommodations for you. You will still start your lessons on Monday with Franklin."

"Really? What's my teacher's name?" Jon asked, his spirits lifting a little.

Mortensen turned away, acting as though he hadn't heard him.

"Professor, who will be my teacher?" Jon repeated. He hated being ignored.

"We will have someone here by Monday, Jonathan, don't worry." But the professor didn't look at him as he said it. Without losing a beat, the man changed the subject to the soccer and track fields they had out back.

Jon followed, dazed and a bit angry. Was there no one like him? How did he already feel so alone in a school of over two hundred students?

Aries House

CHAPTER 7

Frank and Jon would be spending the night in a guest suite with their parents. Mom and Dad were leaving in the morning, and the school was driving them to the airport. But before they were shown to their accommodations, the tour ended along a campus pathway lined with houses. Each house had the school crest on it, as well as its own Zodiac designation.

"I was in the Leo house," Mortensen said, launching nostalgically into a few stories about what it was like to bunk with the same kids every year until he graduated. "You make bonds with other people that you never lose. I'm still friends with everyone I roomed with."

"Mom, what house were you?" Frank asked.

She pointed down the road to a two-story Victorian-style

house, yellow with white shutters. "I was an Aries." She winked at him, and Frank took a good look at the house. It wasn't as well kept as the others; the paint was peeling off the siding, and the stairs up to the door were iffy at best.

"There?" Jon scrunched up his nose.

"The house is old, but it has charm and character," Mom added.

Frank wondered which house he would live in. Would Jon and he be placed in the same house? A wave of nerves rushed through him. He didn't want to be without Jon, to be alone.

"Does it bring back memories, Cece?" Professor Mortensen asked, and Mom nodded.

"It sure does. So many things have changed, but there's so much that hasn't." She looped her arm into Dad's and pointed out a large willow tree near the Aries house. "My favorite reading spot, boys."

Watching Mom share her memories with Dad reminded Frank that soon his parents would be going back to Florida. Jon and he would be left here, in an unfamiliar school, in an unfamiliar state, all the way across the country.

That night, the twins stayed up late and whispered to each other about what they'd seen and learned, but Frank noticed a small change in his brother. Instead of bravado and excitement, there seemed to be some hesitation and even anger. Frank tried not to worry about it too much, brushing it off as he fell asleep.

He was going to miss Mom so much when she left.

∩⌒

The next day, Jon stood back while the driver packed their parents' suitcase into the van. Jon saw his father lean over and whisper something to Professor Mortensen, a serious look on his face. The superintendent's eyebrows raised and a frown appeared on his paling face. Even though he hadn't heard what his dad has said, Jon could guess that his father was making sure his boys would be taken care of. Smirking with pride, Jon puffed his chest out. He wanted to be just as cool as Dad someday.

After her farewells to the professor, Mom turned to him. "Now, Jon, promise your mother that you will behave and listen and tell me all about your adventures when you come home in December." She hugged him. "I love you."

"OK, I love you too, Mom. Tell everyone I say hi."

Mom ruffled his red hair and then swapped twins with Dad.

"Jon"—Dad got down on one knee to look at him—"be safe, and don't get into trouble."

"That's what Mom said," he grunted.

"She knows you well. You do have a knack for

shenanigans." Dad smirked at him, and Jon rolled his eyes, even though he knew it was true. With both hands on Jon's shoulders, his father leaned in and lowered his voice. "Now, listen, if you need us to come back for any reason whatsoever, if something is wrong, I want you to call. OK?"

"Yes, Dad," Jon said.

The two boys watched the van as it pulled away, getting smaller and smaller down the long gravel road. Frank sighed; Jon didn't need telepathy to understand how Frank felt. It was just the two of them now.

"All right boys, let's get you settled in and go over the school rules." Professor Mortensen headed toward the school houses, but even though Jon knew he was supposed to follow, he couldn't take his eyes off the spot where the van had disappeared into the trees. Frank's hand tightened in his, and Jon gave his brother a reassuring squeeze.

They took in a deep breath at the same time.

The professor waited for them a short way down the path, and as they approached, he reached his hand out to Frank. "All right, Franklin, your mother tells me you're wearing a stardust stone. Now that you're at school, it is safe to remove it. We will work through controlling your gift, but in the meantime, let's allow you to experience it."

Frank's hand went straight to the purple sunset stone around his neck. "I don't—"

"It's all right, Franklin." The professor's hand remained outstretched. "It will be given back to you, I promise."

Jon gave him a nod, and Frank cautiously removed the necklace and let the stone and chain drop into the older man's palm. Mortensen placed the necklace in his upper blazer pocket and then waved for the boys to follow him.

Frank felt naked without the stone's weight on his neck, and he dreaded the rush of a school full of thoughts. But everything was quiet.

Your teachers keep it peaceful here. Professor Mortensen eyed him. *You are safe.* "Let's talk about our three major rules," he said out loud. "It's very important that students stay within their appropriate gift level of education. They may expand their abilities with proper supervised instruction, but you must be granted this by myself and the school board. We will do your examinations in your freshman year."

"Why?" Jon asked.

Frank was curious too. Wouldn't they want a gifted student to learn as much as possible, even if their teachers weren't there?

"Gifts are very special, Mr. Reed, but they are also dangerous. As young students, your control over these abilities are still unstable. We want to make sure you can explore your gifts without permanent damage to yourself or others."

Putting his hands behind his back, Mortensen walked past the Capricorn and Aquarius houses. "Our second most important rule is that students cannot use their gifts to cheat, manipulate, or harm anyone. Premeditated crimes of this sort will be harshly dealt with." His voice was firm and tense.

They passed the Pisces and Libra houses. "Of course, there are several forbidden areas but none so guarded as the Sanctuary of Knowledge. No student can enter unless accompanied by a teacher, strictly with my permission.

"Let's just get this straight now." The professor stopped and stared down at them. "I am expecting to never see you in my office for having broken these major rules. There are other rules that you will learn. Some may be harder to follow until you have gained more control over your gifts, but on those rules, we are more flexible." *Even I have broken a few in my time.*

"Oh my . . . Professor Mortensen, you've broken rules?" Frank's eyes got wide.

The professor grimaced at him. "Reading your teacher's mind is one of those rules, young Mr. Reed. You will learn to control it, but try not to do it again. Oh, and we're here…" He pointed behind the boys, and Frank turned to see the yellow-with-white-shutters house and peeling paint.

"Aries? Like—" Jon started.

"Just like Mom," Frank finished. It was the one fact about the house that made it better than all the others. Knowing his mom had been here made him feel closer to her, even though it sure looked as if they hadn't remodeled it since Mom had been in school.

"We were able to place you both in the same house, which was hard to do, since term has already started," Mortensen said.

Frank studied the house he would live in for the rest of his childhood. The three-story building was run down compared to its neighbors, but there were colorful curtains on the windows and a willow tree in the yard.

"Charming and full of character," Frank repeated the phrase, eyeing a large iron symbol of a ram's head, the sign of Aries, nailed to the door.

Professor Mortensen walked up the steps, the boys filing in behind him. A soft knock on the door brought shouts from the other side before the door opened. "Professor Yang?"

The young, petite teacher blinked a couple times, squinting in the sunlight. "Oh, Professor Mortensen." She peered over his shoulder at the twins. "Come in."

"Professor Yang, may I introduce you to your new residents? This is Franklin and Jonathan Reed, Cecelia

McAlister's sons."

"Cece's boys?" Yang grinned. "How wonderful! I'm more than happy to accept new students in our house. I like to have every bed full."

"All right then, boys, I leave you in good hands."

"Now, Franklin and Jonathan, right? I'm Professor Yang, head of Aries house. Why don't you two come in."

She led them into a large living room crowded with mismatched furniture. Every seat seemed to be occupied by kids chatting, playing games on the large coffee tables, or using the computers along the walls.

"Attention, everyone," Yang shouted, clapping her hands. The activity paused as the students glanced up; Franklin felt over two dozen pairs of eyes turn to him. "These are your newest Aries housemates, Franklin and Jonathan. Let's give them a warm Aries welcome. Levan, come on over."

A boy of fourteen or fifteen stood up and reached out a hand to Franklin and Jonathan. "I'm Levan, head boy. Aries is a great house. It may not look as polished as Scorpio's or Virgo's houses, but it is built on our beliefs as a house."

"And what would those be, Levan?" Yang said.

"Aries are independent and natural born leaders," he quoted, holding a hand over his heart. "We are enthusiastic and generous, optimistic and brave. You should be proud to be selected for our house. Come on, I will show you your room and explain the house rules."

Franklin and Jon followed the older student on his tour.

"This is our common room," Levan said. "The computers we use are in the common space. There is restricted access on the computer, but if you need more access, you can get permission from Professor Yang. Common room closes at ten for younger students and midnight for students grade nine and up. Our dorms are up the east staircase. Follow me." Levan headed up, skipping every other step. "What's your gift?"

"I can read thoughts," Frank said.

"Telepathy? Cool! My dad's a telepath." Levan gave him a thumbs-up. "And you?"

"I see things before they happen," Jon answered.

"Really? I haven't met anyone who can do that." His eyebrows raised, as though he was suspicious. "Franklin, right?"

"No, Jonathan, but just Jon is fine."

"Yea, and Frank for me." Frank smiled. "What's your gift?"

"I'm telekinetic." As if to clarify, Levan leaned over the railing on the top floor and waved down to their luggage below, lifting it into the air and up onto the second floor with ease. Frank's and Jon's mouths flew open. "All right, Frank and Jon, let's get you settled in."

Levan led them down a long hallway, floating their luggage behind them, and finally stopped at the very last room. A large number four hung above the door. Their guide tapped once on the door, then opened it to reveal a small room with two sets of bunk beds and two other occupants. "Damien, Nate, come and welcome your new roommates."

Two sets of eyes rose from their books to where Frank and Jon were standing. Right away, Frank noticed the bottom bunks were taken. The first was occupied by a pale brown-haired boy with long legs and boney shoulders. He was sitting against the headboard with his legs awkwardly folded into a crisscross shape. Looking over the top of his book, he gave a lopsided smile in silent greeting.

The other boy had tried hopping out of bed upon their entry, but he'd bumped his head on the top bunk, causing him to drop the comic he'd been reading. Bright and embarrassed eyes stared at them from behind thick black frames as he rubbed his tightly curled black hair.

"Damien and Nate, this is Frank and Jon." Levan flew in the luggage and placed it down gently near the closet.

"Hi, I'm Damien." The clumsy boy picked up his comic and walked closer. "Wait . . . are you two twins? Because you two look exactly the same."

∩∣⌐

"Umm . . . yes," Jon said flatly. When being introduced, they usually received one of two responses: either people were awestruck, or they would annoyingly comment on how adorable they were. He'd rather have the awestruck response.

"I'm Nate." The tall kid shyly nodded from his bed. "Did you want the bottom bunk? I could take a top one if you two want to bunk together."

"Oh no, that's fine," Frank said. "We can both be on the top."

Jon elbowed him, and Frank yelped a little.

Levan smirked. "All right then, I'll get out of your way." On his way out, he glanced back at the twins one more time. "As head boy, I keep the peace around here. If you need anything, you can always ask. I'm three doors down to the right. Welcome, Frank and Jon."

Damien jumped into conversation as soon as Levan closed the door. Bouncing a little on his heels, he rubbed his hands together. "So, which one of you is Frank and which one of you is Jon, again?"

"The taller one is Jon." Frank rolled his eyes over to his brother, and Jon winked back.

"Well, Jon and Frank, welcome to your new home! We're still newbies here too. This is our first year."

"Do you like it?" Frank asked.

Damien shrugged. "As much as a kid could like school."

"I like this school," a quiet voice from the bed answered.

"Well, as much as *most* kids like school," Damien

whispered to Frank.

Nate, the boy on the bed, slowly shook his head, his eyes never leaving his book. He was flipping his pages every twenty seconds or so, which made Jon question if he was actually reading the book at all.

Moving to his luggage, Jon popped the lid open and started to unpack some of his things onto the bunk above Nate. The school allowed them to bring a few personal items. Frank had brought as many comic books as he could, along with his sketch book and pencil set. Jon had brought his baseball glove, ball, and Star Wars action figures. He started putting them one by one on the windowsill by his top bunk: Chewie, Leia, Luke . . . Where was Han?

He'd had Han on the plane . . .

He grabbed his backpack and started frantically dumping everything onto the bedroom floor, mentally retracing his steps.

"What's wrong, Jon?" Frank asked from the bunk across him.

"Han Solo . . . no, Frank, I left him on the plane."

Frank sat up. "What? Are you sure?"

"Yes. I checked everywhere." Jon hung his head, climbing into his bunk and flopping onto his pillow.

"Oh, Jon . . . I'm sorry," Frank said sadly, but he couldn't do anything to fix it.

Interrupting Jon's personal tragedy, a hand popped up from the lower bunk and knocked on the wooden frame near his head. Jon glanced over to see a pair of green eyes looking back at him from under messy brown hair. It made him jump slightly; Nate had been quiet in his approach.

"Sorry, didn't mean to scare you. I did knock," he stuttered.

"I know," Jon said, sitting up.

"I just wanted to say, I'm sorry about your Han Solo. You can have my comic books if you want." The boy put a stack of books onto the bunk, including a few special edition comics Jon hadn't read.

"Oh, thank you." Jon reached for the books, but it didn't feel right. "They're yours. You should keep them."

"No, really," Nate encouraged with a small smile. "I already read them."

"But what if you want to read them again?"

"I only need to read things once. My mom just got these for me." He pointed to a comic. "This one is the best, but I won't tell you how it ends."

"What do you mean you only need to read it once?" Frank asked from his bunk across the room.

"I read *all* my books only once. I can remember all the pictures and words vividly. If I want to read the comic book again, I just close my eyes and see it. It's my gift."

Glancing awkwardly at the twins, Nate slipped down to his lower bunk. Strange kid—but nice. What more could Jon ask for? Maybe at least a teacher!

All Part of the Game

CHAPTER 8

Eating breakfast in the cafeteria wasn't the only thing that was different from Frank's school back home.

At their old school, students didn't wear uniforms. Here Frank had to wear dress pants, a button-up shirt with a collar, and a sweater vest, which was incredibly uncomfortable compared to his normal outfits. A few older students had a different style of uniform, but in general everyone looked the same, like a cohesive group.

But even with the warm sweater vest, Frank was still freezing on the walk to the cafeteria. The weather change from Florida to Washington would be hard to get used to. Though the sun shone outside, a crisp, cold breeze nipped at his skin, and he could see his breath as he walked—something he'd observed in TV shows and movies but never experienced for himself. Fascinated, Frank puffed several times, while Jon pretended he was smoking a pipe.

"Look, I'm good ol' Dr. Harrison," Jon mimicked as they followed the flurry of students to the dining hall.

Fifth grade had several tables in the back; Damien waved at him and Jon from where he was sitting, a sleepy Nate pouring hot sauce onto a plate of eggs and bacon next to him. It was another big change from their old school: rather than sit wherever they wanted, they had to take their meals to a table designated for their age group. At West Hills, there were students from their age all the way to seniors in high school. Frank and Jon had moved from being older kids to among the youngest.

While Frank ate breakfast, he pulled out the wrinkled piece of paper Professor Yang had handed him that morning.

"It is that your schedule?" Damien asked. "I can tell you what we have first. It's social studies. Just follow us after breakfast. All fifthgraders are in the same classes—that is, except for gifts class."

"I see." Frank nodded, rereading the schedule one more time. "So, this afternoon, I meet in the telepathy room for my first gift studies. What about you, Jon?"

Jon was just staring at his paper as if he hadn't heard.

"What is it?"

His brother glanced up, shrugged, and turned his paper

toward Frank. "It says I meet in Professor Mortensen's office this afternoon but will get an updated schedule tomorrow with a firm location."

"Huh, I wonder what that means."

"Perhaps Professor Mortensen is going to be your teacher," Nate suggested, his head popping up from his concentration on his breakfast.

"I don't think so," Jon answered.

Frank had to agree. "He's a telepath. He doesn't even have Jon's gift."

"Then who?" Damien asked. No one knew the answer, but the discussion didn't last much longer. A bell rang, and everyone got up for class.

～)〜

Professor Vidra's students were all seated with their books out when she blew through the door, her red heels clacking on the floor.

"Sorry I'm late!" She grabbed a band around her wrist and pulled her hair into a messy bun on the left side of her head, then began prepping her notes on the desk. Professor Vidra's navy-blue blazer was wrapped over a red button-up shirt and tucked into her rainbow skirt. Jon could have sworn he saw a cat embroidered into the shirt collar around her neck. In keeping with school tradition, though, the school emblem perched like a broach on her right shoulder just above her heart.

"Good morning, class!" she said with a mischievous smile, her voice smooth and comforting. "I hear we have a few new students today, so I'd like to beg all your forgiveness for returning to some topics we've already discussed briefly. If you could all open your books to chapter one."

Many of the students groaned. Nate didn't even open his book; in fact, it didn't look as if he'd brought it with him. Jon pulled out the loaner book the school had given him and opened it to chapter one, which was titled "When the World Thought We Were Magic."

This was going to be a very different social studies than his class back home.

"My dears," Professor Vidra started, "we live in a very different world today than we did a hundred years ago; however, we shouldn't let ourselves become too comfortable. While we have a school, organized society, and an understanding with our government, there is still much that is unsafe for us to share with the general public. The world is still very fearful of our gifts. We must proceed with love and care but also caution."

Several students in the classroom nodded in agreement.

"As we learned in the first chapter, we were once a celebrated race of humans in history." In flowing script,

Vidra wrote several words on the board: Advisor, Dream Interpreter, Prophet, Son of Angels, Wiseman, Seer. "These are only a few beautiful words used to describe what we would do for the world. There were times our people foretold famines and drought. We helped prepare families for hard times. We would solve complex problems and give essential advice to authority.

"History has shown again and again all the accomplishments our people have made. But is has shown some of our most devastating times as well." With a frown, her hands returned to the board: Sorcerer, Witch, Angel of Hell, Demon. "As you can see, these are less flattering terms. Many of our people were killed for the same acts we were once honored for."

Jon listened to the recap of the tragedies that had happened to people like him. Even today, Professor Vidra told them, their people were being put into prisons and asylums for not using their gifts properly or not concealing their true nature.

"I wish, my darlings, I could tell you that the world is not afraid of us, but that would be a lie. And that would not prepare you for the real world." She paused, letting the silence grow heavy. "So, what do we do?"

A girl in the front raised her hand. "We hide?"

"OK, that's one solution. Any more?"

"We move away, isolate ourselves," another student suggested.

A girl sitting in front of Jon shook her head. "Or put ourselves out there, let people know about gifted people."

"No, we fight back. Make them accept us!" a boy from the back shouted.

Professor Vidra leaned forward and pointed at the boy. "Yes Jaylon, we do fight," she said with a mischievous smile, "but not with fists but with words and education. This isn't an old issue, and even though things are better than they were a hundred years ago, there's still so much more to do. This school's one major lesson is kept out in the open: our school's oath. Does anyone know it by heart yet?"

Nate's hand raised. Vidra called him to the front, where he looked blankly at the back wall and started reciting. "As I begin my journey toward understanding of and control over that which I was gifted, I will abide by the rules of the Society of the Perceptually Gifted. I will respect and honor those who teach me and ignore those who try to distract me from our purpose, which is to assist all humankind for the greater good."

Professor Vidra took one of Nathan's hands in hers and then reached her other out to the nearest student. Soon the entire room was holding hands.

Jon did so too, reluctantly. But as soon as Frank gripped

his hand and the chain of students was connected, he didn't regret it anymore. It was as if a current were moving through them, but instead of electricity, it was a shared group emotion: pride for what they stood for, courage, and hope. Jon peered up at his teacher. Her eyes were closed, her breathing slow and relaxed. This feeling—this awesome emotion he'd never experienced before—was somehow being caused by Professor Vidra.

For the last part of the oath, Professor Vidra joined Nathan. "For that which we learn in life to make ourselves stronger must make this world a better place for everyone who shares it."

After class, Jon couldn't stop thinking about the moment they all held hands. Would all his classes be so new and different and thrilling? He couldn't wait to get to his next class, English.

But, sadly, he'd been set up for disappointment. Professor Owens turned out to be the most ill-tempered teacher he'd ever had, the total opposite of Professor Vidra.

"I was told there were two new students in this class. I want to start off by saying I am not accommodating your late-term admittance. You will have to catch up before December break, and I am expecting you to turn in your first paper tomorrow along with the others in class. Now that the nonsense is over, let's get back on topic. Turn your books to page twenty-five."

Though English was usually one of Jon favorite subjects, after meeting Professor Owens, he realized this year was going to be different. Owens spent the two-hour period making snide comments about proper grammar and a certain student's inability to spell. As snobby as Owens was, Jon couldn't help but chuckle as he nudged Frank's elbow. "He's your gifts teacher."

His brother made a face at him. "Laugh it up. You don't even know who your teacher is."

The comment was meant as a joke, but it stung, as if his brother had punched him in the chest. Jon refused to speak to Frank as they walked to their next class.

What if Frank was right? What if his teacher was horrible? Or worse yet, what if there was no one to help him?

Quickly following Damien and Nate, they headed toward the locker rooms to change for PE. On the court, a sign directed their class to the soccer field outside.

Jon gawked at Professor Yang twirling a soccer ball above her head with a twist of her finger. It took everything in him not to test the ball for strings or jump up and pull it down. Was he ever going to get used to seeing such things?

"All right, everyone," Yang interrupted the amusement to address the group. "Let's break you up into two teams. Today we're going to have a soccer scrimmage. Kevin, Esther, let's have you start us off."

A tall thin boy and a girl with short blonde hair came forward, next to Yang.

Soccer! Jon couldn't wait to show his fellow classmates all his skills; he'd been considered the best athlete—especially in soccer—at his old school. He took pride in being a fast and bold player, willing to take those impossible shots for a goal, and even though Frank was more reserved on the field, they did make a pretty good team together.

The twins were both selected to play on Kevin's team. Professor Yang handed out worn, musty net vests to each team, and Jon quickly pulled on his blue practice vest. The other team was sporting neon yellow.

Kevin, as captain, got to split up the students into positions. As there was fourteen of them, Kevin chose three smaller fifth graders to be substitutes. Jon was placed in the forward position after sharing his previous soccer experience, and Frank was chosen as a midfielder.

Blue team won the coin toss, and Professor Yang blew the whistle for kickoff.

The starter kid kicked the ball toward Jon. Trapping it with the toes of his shoe, he started dribbling it up the field. To his left, someone shouted that they were open, but Jon ignored them. His focus was solely on the goal in front of him and the players trying to block him.

Dodging a couple midfielders, Jon nudged fairly hard into a defender and knocked her to the ground. He finally had an opening for the goal. With a risky shot, he kicked the ball and watched it soar past the bulky yellow-team goalie. Blue team cheered and gave him high fives to celebrate.

Pumped and on the way back to his starting position, he saw the defender still sitting on the ground. Her whole left side was covered in wet dirt, and her hazel brown skin was smeared from where she'd tried to wipe the mud away. She tried to stand but slipped onto her backside, her wavy brown ponytail bouncing.

Jon reached a hand to her. "Sorry about that. All part of the game, huh?"

A pair of intense honey-colored eyes shot a glare at him. "I can get up just fine on my own," she said through gritted teeth. She shook out her hands, and the mud that was still clinging slopped back onto the field. Jon shrugged at her and took off.

They kicked off again. This time it was yellow's ball. Jon's opponents dribbled for several minutes, passing back and forth into blue territory. Frank struggled to get the ball from one of yellow's forwards, but eventually he managed to side-kick it into an open space on the field.

Jon rushed forward to retrieve it, and he started dribbling toward the yellow team's goal again. To his surprise, the field was wide open, and he pushed forward with a rush of adrenaline, not bothering to scan his surroundings. He didn't realize his error until something hit the ball out from under him and he tripped, his whole body flying forward, flipping and sliding into the muddy field.

Shocked, he lifted his face from the mud, spitting out bits of grass and dirt. He tried to push himself up, but it was wet and slippery, so he had to roll over into a sitting position first. Down the field, he spotted the defender, who had just finished booting the ball upfield to her team. She turned around and smirked at him.

"All part of the game, right?" she called.

Jon sat in shock for a moment, pounded the ground in frustration with one fist, then asked for a substitute.

PE ended with a tie between blue and yellow.

"Wow Jon." Frank laughed as they headed to the showers. "I didn't know your gift was flying."

The other boys chuckled.

"Yeah, wow, she really did a great slide tackle," Damien said next to him. "Aimed directly for the ball and took Jon out as a bonus."

The laughter started again, but Jon wasn't laughing. He still ached and was completely covered in mud.

"Who was that?" Frank asked, and even though Jon was upset, he couldn't help but be curious too.

"Not sure. I think her name is Melanie or Miley or something," Damien said. "I haven't met her yet."

They ate with Kevin—the classmate who'd captained the blue team—and reminisced on their PE scrimmage. Jon wished they had more opportunities to play throughout the day.

"There is a soccer and basketball league here," Kevin said. "You can try out for the teams but only within your cohort group."

"What does that mean?" Damien asked.

"It means if you're in the Leo house, you go to where the Leo house has tryouts. There's a schedule when tryouts start. Usually two different houses are represented on each team," Kevin said, his mouth full of spaghetti.

"How do you know?" Frank asked.

"My older sister plays on a team. She's in the Sagittarius house like me, which means our teams have students from both our house and the Virgo house."

Jon's ears had perked up as soon as Kevin mentioned getting on a team. "When are the tryouts?"

"Not sure. But don't get too excited, usually fifth graders aren't picked. We just aren't as good as the tenth and twelfth graders."

Kevin sighed, but Jon smirked. He enjoyed challenges. Who knew, maybe he would make school history as one of the youngest players?

Gifts Class

CHAPTER 9

As the students filed into the large library after lunch, Professor Wyatt was perched at his desk, his feet propped up, his eyes scurrying over the thick book in his hands. He jumped at their entrance and quickly straightened his papers.

"Good morning, professor," Nathan said as they walked by him.

Wyatt simply nodded, silently watching the students take their seats. Professor Wyatt was a tall, lanky man who didn't have to clear his throat or address the class to get their attention. In fact, as soon as everyone sat down, the room went completely silent.

Soon Frank realized why: Professor Wyatt was a mumbler. Even though the class was being tiptoe quiet, several students still had to ask him to repeat everything he said. Every time the professor was asked a question, he had a quirk of adjusting his large-frame glasses and saying the answer quietly to himself before repeating louder.

"Please bring out last week's homework for review," he said a third time. He seemed unbothered by the constant requests for him to repeat himself; the students didn't seem impatient either.

Professor Wyatt spent most of class talking to the white board and reviewing math problems. It was easy for Frank to understand the concepts once he saw the solutions.

The other unconventional thing about math class, besides Professor Wyatt, was a group of six students sitting off to the right. Each one appeared to be working independently through a large amount of additional math worksheets. Their roommate Nate was one of them.

Later, before their next period, Frank had to ask him what they were doing.

"Sagacity students usually move at a much faster pace, according to Professor Wyatt. He gives us additional work so we don't get bored."

Frank nodded. If you were incapable of forgetting anything you read, it made sense you would learn more quickly.

Frank was still getting used to going to different periods; it made him feel like a middle schooler or high schooler. Back home, they had one classroom and one teacher for all subjects.

Science class started off well. Frank and Jon sat with their roommates during lab. Damien slowly measured things for their experiment while everyone else took notes or read the instructions.

Professor Gonzalez glided slowly from table to table, checking on each lab group's progress. For a while, Frank felt as if science class was the most normal thing he'd done all day—until the incident.

"Professor," a girl in front of them said, "I can't use this." She pointed to the bowl in front of her. "Its vibes are . . ."

The girl shook her head, and her friend pushed the bowl away, but it was too late.

The girl's eyes rolled back in her head, and she started to shake violently. Professor Gonzalez barely made it in time to catch her before she collapsed to the floor. Was she having a seizure?

Frank couldn't stop staring, his stomach turning. Their professor called into the hall, and a staff member came to help carry the girl out.

"Where are they taking her?" Jon asked their group.

"Probably the school medical center," Damien said with a frown.

Frank's mouth felt dry. "That was scary. What happened?"

"New students, even me," Nate said quietly, "we're still not able to control everything that's happening to us. Iffah is a psychic. She can sense energy from things. I think the bowl had some bad energy."

"Reminded me of when you had to leave class. I failed that test thinking about you," Jon murmured for only Frank to hear. When Frank glanced over at his brother, he saw a slight haunted look in his eyes. Maybe Jon wasn't as brave as he appeared.

Professor Gonzalez came back into the room and wrapped the offending bowl in a towel, handing it to another staff member.

"I heard it only gets more and more frequent as we get older," Damien added. "That's why we have to learn to control it. That isn't the first time either. A kid in my gifts class had an episode the first week and was taken to the medical center."

Frank nodded, remembering his own episodes of uncontrol. The random voices had been much less frequent since they'd arrived at school, but there was still an annoying buzz in his head.

"Gifts class? What is your gift, Damien?" Jon asked, and it hit Frank; they'd never asked their new roommate.

"My gift? Oh, I'm an . . ." He grumbled something Frank didn't understand.

"What was that?" Jon asked, and they both leaned in closer to hear.

"I'm an . . ." Damien looked embarrassed but finally sighed, glancing at them over his glasses. "I'm an empath."

"Empath? Isn't that what Mom's gift is?" Jon asked Frank.

"Yes, it is. Cool."

Damien looked up in surprise. "Really? Because to me, it doesn't sound all that cool."

"My mom's an empath, and she is the coolest person I know," Frank said. "Why would it not be?"

Damien looked down again.

Nate patted him on the back. "Some people tease empaths for being too sensitive, and there are some who think if you're sensitive, it affects how strong you are as a person. But it isn't true, Damien." Nathan smiled, but Frank could see Damien wasn't convinced.

"Well, we think it's an awesome gift. You should be proud." Frank smiled too.

Finally, Damian gave a small smirk back. "OK, friend."

Friend. Frank's first friend at school. Since leaving Carver and Elena back home, he'd been worried about making new friends. But he'd already made at least two, and it was only the second day. Perhaps this new school wouldn't be so scary after all.

∩⌒

After science class, Jon said goodbye to Frank and went to meet with Professor Mortensen in his office by the assembly hall. Outside the door, he took a deep breath and knocked, and a voice inside told him to enter.

When Jon cracked the door open, another person was already sitting in the chair in front of Professor Mortensen's desk. Mortensen nodded to the man and stood to greet Jon.

"Mr. Reed," Mortensen said, "I'd like you to meet your new teacher, Professor McClery."

The stranger had been loudly tapping his wooden cane against the ground, but he paused as he used it to stand, clasping the cane's golden knob in front of him. He had a wide frame and was slightly bent over from either age or hard work. His reddish-brown beard and hair were speckled with white, and he was wearing a tan blazer and flat capped gray hat.

There was something overwhelming about his new teacher's presence; Jon wasn't sure exactly what. Was it the thick beard that encompassed most of his face, or was it the man's sharp narrowed eyes?

"It's nice to meet you," Jon said quietly and put his hand out to shake, but Professor McClery didn't return the gesture. His eyes stayed fixed on Jon, scrutinizing closely. It made Jon feel young and insignificant.

"What's its name again?" McClery said to Professor Mortensen, as if Jon weren't there. His husky voice had a strong Irish accent.

"Reed. Jonathan Reed," Mortensen said.

"All right, Mister Ree-ed." McClery drew Jon's last name out with a grumpy tone. "Follow me then." McClery passed him, leaning on his cane and limping slightly.

Professor Mortensen grinned nervously at Jon but didn't offer any comfort. Sucking it up, Jon lifted his chin and followed the older man out the door.

They left the main school building by way of the front stairs and continued down a pathway.

"Sir, where are we going?" Jon asked, but the man beside him only grunted. Jon hated being ignored, but he was too nervous and confused to say anything. Their strangely silent walk ended at a small cottage on the edge of the school property. McClery pulled an old skeleton key out of his pocket and jimmied the lock a bit before opening the door.

"There is no classroom available for your lessons," McClery grumbled as he pocketed the key and shuffled inside, "so we will be using this house for the time being."

Jon walked in and let his eyes get accustomed to the dark interior. Where was the light switch? McClery pulled a curtain back from the front window, the daylight illuminating swirls of dust.

It was obvious the house had been empty for some time. Cobwebs stuck to the corners and around the furniture, all draped in white sheets. The windowsills and mantel were covered in a thick layer of dirt.

"Now, first things first," McClery said, "do not call me professor. I am not a professor. You may call me *sir* and *sir* only. Is that clear?" He waited for Jon to acknowledge him with a nod, then limped into the nearest chair by the window. A small dust plume erupted from it as he sat down. "Now, boy, tell me about this gift of yours."

Jon coughed as dust drifted into his mouth. "Well, I sometimes know things will happen before they happen."

"Sometimes?" It was that tone again, the one that made him feel small, stupid. "What term of measurement is *sometimes*? One, two, eleven times?"

"Well—"

"And how long before what you predict happens? One second, three minutes, a couple of years?" The man glared at him intensely.

"Well, I don't know, sir—"

"Ha!" McClery laughed, annoyed, and flung his hand out in front of him. "This is who I'm teaching? A boy who can barely tell what time it is, let alone the future."

Jon swallowed. There was silence for several minutes.

Though McClery's eyes were thoughtful, his mouth twisted into a small smirk. "Before we move on, tell me one thing you predicted."

"Um, I saw my brother was going to get sick, and he did—"

"Stop there!" The man's booming voice made Jon jump. McClery's expression had changed; his eyebrows knitted as he leaned forward. "I need to know everything, Jon. Not just what happened but how it happened. What did it feel like? What did you see?"

Jon stopped himself from anxiously chewing on his nails. This man was insane. They'd given him a crazy teacher; he was sure of it. But there was nothing he could do but cooperate. He closed his eyes, trying to replay the scene in his head.

"I woke from a bad dream, and my little brother was over me, telling me I was talking in my sleep. I heard crying, but no one was crying. I saw a shadow above my brother, Franklin, in his bed, like a ghost of him, and it was upset. I saw a shadow of my parents coming into our room, but our bedroom door was closed. Then a minute or so later, it happened, just as I saw it."

When he opened his eyes, he was slightly disturbed to see McClery studying him as if he were an interesting book.

"This bad dream that woke you, do you remember what it was?" McClery asked pointedly. Jon felt as if the man's eyes were burning into his skin.

"No," Jon lied. He wasn't sure what the dream *meant* anyway, and it wasn't any of this man's business.

"Hmmm . . ." After what seemed an eternity, the older

man leaned back in his chair and stared at the golden knob of his cane. "All right, Mr. Reed. I will take your case."

Had this been some kind of test?

"Your first lesson starts today." McClery pointed to the furniture around the room. "Lesson one, I want you to clear the sheets off of every piece of furniture in this house, you got it?"

"Sir, I don't understand."

McClery's stern look brooked no arguments. "This isn't up for negotiations, Mr. Reed."

Jon shook his head, clenching his fists. This was definitely not the type of instruction he'd expected from his new teacher. Being assigned cleaning as schoolwork made no sense.

Quickly, Jon stomped through the house pulling sheets off, fueled by the boiling in his stomach. He piled up every sheet in the living room until the stack was as tall as he was. When he was finished, he stood in front of McClery, his breathing rapid.

"Done," he said sharply.

McClery smirked. "All right, Mr. Reed, you may go."

"What?" Jon's voice cracked into a whine. "What about the rest of my lesson?"

"That was your first lesson," McClery said calmly. "You are a very unique boy, Mr. Reed, and require a very specific course. Now, I won't say it again. You may go."

Jon grabbed his backpack and slammed the door behind him. With loud, raging stomps, he marched back to Aries house and up to his bed.

It was quiet inside. Everyone was still in their lessons.

Everyone but him.

Food Fight!

CHAPTER 10

Franklin and his new friends hurried back to Aries house after school.

"Hey, Frank, you wanna go hiking with us on the trails behind the school?" Damien asked. "I've been dying to explore them."

Frank grudgingly declined; he didn't have time. Professor Owens had slammed him with a month's worth of English homework, not including the paper that was due the next day.

Professor Owens's other class—Frank's gift class—hadn't been easy either. He'd walked into a room full of kids he didn't know, each with the gift of telepathy, and found an empty chair across from a girl named Paige.

During the first hour, Professor Owens had assigned them

to work in pairs. Frank was supposed to ask Paige a question out loud, and she was supposed to answer telepathically; then they would trade places. Frank had spent the whole forty-five minutes trying to read her mind to find out what type of cookies she liked. By the end of class, he still didn't know, even though Paige had been able to get through two questions.

While Frank had read minds without trying dozens of times, doing it purposefully was turning out to be very hard.

"It's OK." Paige gave him a pitying smile. "I've been practicing. You'll get there! Try practicing at your house. You just need willing participants."

He'd thanked her for the advice, hoping tomorrow would be different.

When they arrived back at their room, Jon was already lying on his bunk, tossing his baseball up in the air and catching it with his mitt.

"Hey, Jon, how was your class?"

"Awful," he responded. "I think I got a military general as my gifts teacher." Moaning, he peered over the bunk's edge. "How was yours?"

"I have a lot of homework."

"Well, we better eat dinner and get to it." Jon climbed down from the top bunk.

Once they returned from dinner in the cafeteria, Jon and

Frank headed to the Aries house common area to work on their English papers. Nat and Damien had already finished their homework but were nice enough to help.

"Go ahead, ask me a question about the chapter. I can answer it verbatim," Nate offered.

Frank didn't know what *verbatim* meant, but that didn't stop him from taking advantage of Nate's knowledge. A couple hours later, both he and Jon had decent papers written for English and had completed the math practice page for tomorrow's lesson. Unfortunately, it was already getting dark outside, and there were only a few minutes left until curfew. Frank shook his head in frustration. They had lost their opportunity to explore the school trails.

"Well, if we can't go out, Jon, can I practice my telepathy on you?" Frank asked, remembering Paige's advice.

"Sure." Jon shrugged. "What do I need to do?"

"Oh, cool!" Damien said from his spot on the floor. "I've never seen a telepathy exercise before."

"Me either." Nate moved next to Damien for a better view. Jon and Frank sat across from each other on the couches.

"I'll ask you a question, and you answer in your head—*only* in your head. Don't say it out loud, OK?" Frank pulled out his worksheet.

Jon nodded. "Got it."

"OK, what is your favorite cookie?"

Jon snorted. "Frank, you already know what my favorite cookie is."

"Yeah, I bet you guys know everything about each other." Damien narrowed his eyes at Frank, as if he thought he was cheating. "You have to ask him something you don't know."

Frank looked down at his paper and then back up to his twin, who wore an amused smirk. What was something he didn't already know about Jon? As he pressed his fingers to his forehead, thinking hard, it came to him.

"What's your new teacher's name? Just think the name over and over in your head." That was what Professor Owens had suggested the silent partner do, repeat the word over and over. Frank prepared his mind, breathing in and out slowly just as they'd done in class. *Focus on his thoughts, Frank*, he told himself as he stared at his brother. *Mc. . . McL . . . McClery*. "Is it McClery?"

Jon's eyes got wide. "Yeah, it is. Great job, Frank! Go ahead ask me another one."

"OK." Frank smiled, feeling impressed with himself. For some reason reading Jon's mind was easy compared to reading Paige's. "What does your teacher look like?"

Jon's answer was more jumbled this time; then it hit Frank in a rush, as if flying through space into his brain.

"An old man?"

Jon nodded and smiled.

Damien laughed and rocked backward. "That was great! Another! Another!"

"Jon, what did you learn from McClery today?" As Frank asked the question, Jon's face fell. His smile disappeared, his brows creased, and he sucked in a deep breath. *Oh gosh, Frank, don't ask me that, please.*

"Why not?" Frank answered without thinking. He almost hadn't realized Jon's mouth hadn't moved except to make a deeper frown.

"Congratulations, Frank, you read my mind," Jon said sharply.

"What did he say?" Damien asked. Neither boy answered. Frank wasn't going to repeat it after Jon's reaction. "Wait, Frank, what did he say?"

Jon stood up. "OK, guys, show's over. I hope it helped, Frank. I'm going to bed."

Frank sighed as Jon grabbed his backpack and headed upstairs. His brother was hiding something. But why?

∩⌒

For the next two weeks, Jon never once talked with Frank about his lessons with McClery. It would be pointless conversation anyway; he hadn't done anything except clean an old house. Jon's second lesson had been to clear away all the cobwebs with a broom. Letting his anger get the best of him, Jon had barely scraped the broom bristles on the walls, and only to where he could easily reach. When the General—Jon's new nickname for McClery—had inspected his work and deemed it unsatisfactory, he hadn't released Jon from lessons until it was fixed.

And even that hadn't been so bad. The worst thing was that McClery had now formed a habit of following him around at school. It was as if the man *wanted* to unnerve him.

During PE, Jon spotted McClery's tan blazer and cane on the soccer field sidelines. A nasty glare was crusted on the older man's features. It unsettled Jon enough to throw his game completely off. He took the ball from his own team member, Kevin, and with haphazard control, shot at the goal and missed.

The PE team was upset at him, Kevin was angry with him, and he was livid with himself.

This didn't improve Jon's attitude. By that Friday evening, Nate and Damien were stepping on eggshells around him, and Frank had stopped talking to him.

He couldn't help but feel lonely, but he also couldn't stop the constant frustration bubbling inside him all the time, ready to burst out at the slightest chance. At one point, he tripped over Nate's laundry and went off on him for leaving it on the floor.

"What's your problem?" Frank finally asked in the cafeteria that night. "You've been acting like a jerk for over a week. And what you said to Nate today, about cleaning up his stuff? Since when have you cared about keeping things clean?"

"Look, Frank"—Jon turned to his brother, who was standing behind him holding an empty dinner tray—"why don't you just read my mind and figure it out. Since your gift is almighty and all."

Jon shoved his own tray into the tray return and skirted past his brother, but a wave of dizziness pulled him up short. He swayed on his feet as the room seemed to twist.

"Jon?" Frank's voice sounded as if it were underwater.

Then it happened again—shadows. Shadow figures, like one he'd seen in his old bedroom, but this time it was a shadow of a girl walking. Another shadow figure appeared and bumped into her, knocking her to the ground so her tray of food landed in her lap.

Something about the last shadow figure looked familiar.

A muddled voice was calling his name, and the shadows vanished. Someone's hands were on his shoulder and elbow, holding him up.

"Jon, you OK?" Frank asked. He looked concerned.

"I'm fine!" Shrugging Frank off, Jon took two quick steps—and crashed right into someone walking to the tray return.

"Hey! What the—?" the person yelled as they fell to the floor.

Jon pulled back, his mouth hanging open. The girl he'd run into was no longer a shadow figure but a physical person. Her plate of leftover food was decorating the front of her uniform.

She pressed her lips together in annoyance, glaring at him. Jon swallowed; it was the same girl he'd pushed into the mud his first week.

"Sorry," Jon said, his heart racing a little as he watched her fume.

"It's OK . . ." she said calmly, but her tone was sarcastic. A nearby friend helped her slowly to her feet. "I guess I just can't keep a clean uniform around you."

"I, umm . . ." Jon was going to apologize again, but he was interrupted by a handful of mashed potatoes smacking into his chest. The girl laughed as she smeared the rest of her goopy leftovers onto his uniform.

Jon, too shocked to move, could do nothing but watch. The girl winked at him as a couple more students at her table raised their trays of food too.

"Wait!" Frank moved to block Jon from their attack. "It was an accident—" But slushy mashed potatoes hit him in the face like a snowball.

"Food fight!" yelled Damien as he grabbed what was leftover on his plate.

Chaos erupted in the cafeteria. Even though it had started at the fifth-grade table, the sixth and seventh graders quickly joined in with their own methods of attack. Many students ran for the doors, while others scrambled to combine what ammunition they could find. For the first time in almost a month, Jon chuckled. His laugh only grew as Frank wiped potatoes from his face and stared at him. Soon, Frank couldn't hold back his chuckles either.

Grabbing his brother's hand, Jon pulled him under a table. "All right, you're on collections. I've got targeting."

"Sniper?" Frank whispered.

"Yes. Can you find me more meatloaf?"

Frank nodded and left, returning quickly with several half-eaten pieces. Jon searched under the table until he found a spoon and fork. *Perfect.* As Frank massaged the meatloaf pieces into small balls, Jon placed them on the fork, drawing on years of practice for high-precision aiming. Meatloaf balls started flying from their corner. Jon pumped his fist as one hit a larger eighth-grader on the shoulder.

A loud, booming voice gave Jon his next target. He pulled his fork back like a catapult and let the meatloaf ball fly. It soared through the air and landed with a small splat.

"Yes!" Jon jumped up to see his victory hit. His voice

echoed through the suddenly silent room.

"Mister Reeeeeed!" A piece of meatloaf was dangling from Professor Owens's mustache.

"Oh gosh, Jon, it's not who I think it is, is it?" Frank asked from under the table.

Jon felt the blood drain from his face.

"Get out here!" Professor Owens commanded, and Frank crawled out to stand by his brother. "All right," Owens asked the standing crowd of students, "who started this?"

A dozen or so fingers pointed to Jon, Frank, and the brown-haired girl next to them.

Owens stomped slowly over to them, his face red as the meatloaf ketchup smeared on his cheek. "You three stay . . ." He paused menacingly, then glanced at the crowd of students. "Everyone else, leave the premises. If I see any of you here in the next minute, you'll get the same punishment as these three."

The cafeteria was instantly vacated; soon they and Professor Owens were the only ones left. "You haven't been here for even a month, and you've already disrupted this school, boys. And you, Miss Camacho"—he narrowed his pudgy eyes at the girl—"I have better expectations for you considering your family."

"Sorry, professor," she said quietly.

"Now, you will all stay here no matter how late it gets

and clean this entire cafeteria. I will be reporting all your behavior to the superintendent for continued disciplinary actions." He stomped off to the janitorial closet and seized the mops and rags, shoving them into their hands. "Until it is *spotless*. Understand?"

Jon studied the disaster around the room. Not only was food splattered on the walls, but it laced every chair and hung loosely from the ceiling. It would take hours to clean this up. Jon sighed; it felt like gift lessons all over again.

"Professor Owens," an Irish-accented voice said from the doorway. Jon's head shot up, his eyes widening—*McClery!* "Let me stay with them."

"Are you sure?" Owens asked.

McClery limped over with his cane, observing the students with a smirk. "Get yourself cleaned up. You know I'll make sure it's spotless."

Owens nodded and took one last disapproving glare at the boys before leaving.

Jon's stomach churned. Having Owens oversee their cleanup would have been awful, but having McClery would be a nightmare.

"All right, you must be Franklin." McClery leaned on his cane as he stared at Frank. Jon was surprised the older man could tell them apart. Not even Professor Yang had gotten them straightened out yet. "And you, my dear, are

Miss Camacho."

"Yes, sir." She lifted her chin.

"All right then, get to it." They all hesitated, momentarily unsure if he was talking to them. "Well, off ya go!" he shouted, which startled them into moving.

"I'll take the ceiling." Jon already had practice from doing it in the cottage earlier in the week. "Frank, you take the rag to the walls, and you—"

"I am not 'you.' My name is Mira." She crossed her arms.

"Mira, can you do tables?" Jon asked politely. He needed her cooperation if they were going to finish before midnight. She looked ready to retort, but then Jon added, "If you want to. Unless you have a better plan?" He really didn't want to make an enemy.

She sighed. "I can do tables."

As they all started cleaning, Jon could feel McClery's eyes on his back. The ceiling took forever; Jon was careful not to make the mess worse for the others working below.

Several hours later, the ceiling was clean, the walls and tables were spotless, and the chairs were being wiped down by both boys as Mira mopped the floor. They paused once for inspection, but McClery told them to keep going until he said to stop.

Jon was sore, Frank was sweating, and Mira looked as if she was about to fall over when McClery finally said, "All right, you may go." He took the cleaning supplies, and they skirted out before he could change his mind.

It was dark and cold outside as they walked to their houses. Curfew was long past, and Jon rubbed his shoulders to keep warm. His jacket wasn't enough to keep out the chill, especially with the water, soap, and food soaked through his clothing.

Mira finally broke the silence. "Who was that guy?"

"The General," Jon said without a smile.

Mira stopped and stared at him. "Excuse me?"

"That's what I call him."

"Professor McClery is Jon's gifts teacher," Frank added.

"Ha! If you can call him a teacher," Jon said on a groan, finally letting it all out. "What we did tonight, that's what I do every day for him."

"What?" Frank and Mira said at the same time, shocked.

"You clean for him?"

"Yeah," Jon said. It felt nice to admit it, to have others around who'd also experienced McClery's brutal attitude. "He hasn't actually taught me anything about my gift."

"What is your gift?" Mira asked, and when Jon told her, she became quiet. "That's very rare."

"That's what everyone says."

They continued to walk in awkward silence for a while until Mira finally spoke up. "You both smell awful."

"Well you're no pile of roses," Jon remarked, and they all smiled at each other and began to laugh.

The secret valley

CHAPTER 11

Frank was thankful to see Jon in a better mood after the food fight and the cleanup, even though it had exhausted them.

They hadn't gotten back to their room until almost ten o'clock last night. Even after they'd showered, the smell of cleaner and meatloaf had still lingered. Damien complained a little, but eventually they all toughed out the smell and got to sleep.

The next morning Levan woke them up and told them to report to Professor Mortensen's office at ten.

Saturdays and Sundays were the only days they didn't have to wear their uniforms, so they both dressed in T-shirts, jeans, and warm sweaters. After breakfast, they met Mira on their way to Mortensen's office.

Frank knocked, and a voice inside told them to come in.

Mortensen was sitting behind his desk, and a tall, grumpy-looking woman wearing an apron was standing off to the left. She looked down her nose at them as they entered.

"Oh, yes, boys and Miss Camacho, this is Gertrude Sniffens. She is our chef and kitchen manager. Mrs. Sniffens will be getting a few extra hands in the kitchen to help clean and prep food after dinner every night for the next week. Isn't that right, Mrs. Sniffens?"

"Oh, yes, I'm looking forward to it. It can be a long night." Her sinister smile made Frank flinch. Mrs. Sniffens was missing several teeth, which caused her to spit a little as she talked.

Mortensen wrote something on a piece of paper. "Perhaps this will help you understand and appreciate the hard work people put into making meals around here. What do you have to say to Mrs. Sniffens?"

"We're sorry," Frank said, and the others nodded.

"Report for duty at exactly six thirty," Mrs. Sniffens ordered, then swished from the room with a grunt.

"I'm also writing up official letters to your parents and for your school records. Be aware, boys, we do not take mischief like this lightly. Miss Camacho, I believe I don't need to remind you about school rules. I'm sure your father will have enough to say on the school's behalf. You're dismissed."

As they walked outside, Jon turned around with a smile.

"That wasn't so bad. A week of kitchen duty? It was so worth it."

"Worth it?" Mira's face was pale. "That's the first time I've ever gotten into trouble, and it's all thanks to you, Jonathan Reed. Oh no, my dad is going to kill me."

"Wait," Frank asked, amazed, "how did you know he was Jonathan and not me?"

Mira put her hands on her hips. "Because he's the jerk, and you're not."

"I'm a jerk?" Jon laughed, making a mock hurt look.

"Yes, you are a jerk. At PE you take the ball from your own players and you plow people down. You don't care about sportsmanship or teamwork—just about winning. That doesn't make you a good player. It just makes you a jerk." Mira folded her arms over her chest.

"Really? Frank, do you think so?"

Frank didn't say anything; he wasn't sure Jon would like his answer. His brother had been on a short fuse the last week and very unlike himself.

"I don't want to be a jerk," Jon said quietly. "I'm sorry, Mira."

"Really sorry? Or 'sorry but it was worth it' sorry?"

"Really sorry."

To Frank, it sounded legit.

"Hmm . . ." Mira looked him up and down. "We'll see.

Now be less like a jerk."

"Yes, ma'am."

"Oh, you got told!" Frank laughed. Jon nudged him, and Mira chuckled.

"OK then. Now let's enjoy our Saturday, since we're probably not going to get many evenings off in the next week." Mira walked past them, swishing her hair back into a bun. "Hey, you want to see something cool?"

"Yeah," they both responded, and to Frank's surprise, Mira grabbed both their hands and led them toward the outskirts of school.

"Where are we going? The trails?" Jon asked.

Mira giggled and shook her head as she continued to drag them toward the forest. "Aren't the best things in the world surprises? You'll see, it's even better. There is no trail to this place." Mira let them both go and started walking into the forest, off the path. "Be careful, the undergrowth is thick, and there are tree branches that hide under it. Easy tripping hazard."

Mira moved fast, and Frank had to scramble to keep up. Trees in Washington were so different from in Florida. When Frank took a moment to breathe, resting his hand against a large evergreen, sap instantly caught his skin. The bark was rough and knotted, and he couldn't even see the top from where he was standing. It must have been twelve stories high.

"Come on, Franky," Jon said from up ahead.

The forest started going up a hill, which became steeper as they climbed. Frank held on to the tree branches for balance.

"Are we there yet?" he called out to Mira, who was several yards ahead of him.

"Almost!" Mira yelled. "Come on!"

Once Frank made it to the top, he leaned on his knees to catch his breath. The view was incredible—like an illustration out of a fantasy book. In a valley a little way below them was a clearing surrounded by rolling green hills. Behind it, towering like a god, was a huge snowcapped mountain in front of stark blue skies.

Mira glanced over her shoulders to wink at them. "What? You two look lost. Never seen a mountain before?"

"I guess not as much as you have," Jon retorted.

"Well, if you like that, you'll love this. Look down there . . ." Mira pointed, drawing Frank's attention to a huge statue in the clearing below. It was too far away to really make out the details.

Putting a hand up to still them, Mira walked to the base of large oak and dug through a pile of underbrush. Slowly, she pulled out a large roll of plastic sheeting, which he noticed was tied with rope to the tree trunk. She dropped the sheeting down the hill, letting it roll out all the way to the clearing.

"Whoa, a slide!" Jon pumped the air with both fists.

"Where did you get that?" Frank asked with astonishment.

Mira smiled proudly. "I don't reveal my sources. Here, take off your coats." Mira slipped her jacket off, placed it on the makeshift slide, and sat down. "Geronimo!"

She flew down the slide with dizzying speed, tumbling at the end with a laugh. Frank and Jon quickly tore their coats off and, one after another, slid down to meet her. Mira was pulling her jacket back on and brushing leaves off her pants when Frank hit the bottom.

He rubbed his backside a little. "I must had hit a rock."

"Watch out below!" Jon yelled right before he rammed into Frank. Laughing, Frank pushed him off, and they started wrestling a little until Mira lightly knocked their heads together.

"Knock it off and come on."

Frank shimmied his jacket on, shook the twigs out of his hair, and stood to follow. Now that they were in the clearing, he could finally get a good look at the statue in the middle. It was at least thirty feet tall and depicted a man sitting on a stone, his arms stretched out, palms open, eyes staring into the woods. On his bare chest was the school symbol—the symbol Frank had seen on the door above the school, on the emblem of their school uniforms. The sun with the eye in it.

"Wow," Jon said.

"Yeah," Frank agreed. The statue appeared old, with long vines and mounds of moss growing on its bronze-like exterior. As the twins approached, Frank tripped on what he thought was a stone, but when he backed up, he realized it was actually a round plaque. In fact, there were plaques all the way around the statue; he counted seven in total. Each one showed a different symbol.

"Do you like it?" Mira asked as she climbed on the statue's bottom half. "I found it last summer all on my own. I haven't taken anyone else up here yet!"

"How?" Frank asked.

Jon followed her up. "What is it?"

"I just found it, OK? I think it's from the poem of the old man. You know the one."

"No."

"Oh . . . well, it goes like this:

'There once was a fearful old man
who couldn't keep Darkness away,
So he stole from his friends six secret jars
To extend his life for a day.

He opened oracles, psychics, and telepaths,
Pouring them all in a pot.

He mixed in kinetics, sages, and empaths,
Heating it to boiling hot.

As Darkness approached, the old man panicked.
He drank from his pot of six gifts.
Then Light raced in and took them both,
Its exit brilliant and swift.'"

"So, he died anyway?"

"Yeah, my dad said the moral of the story is that we have only one gift for a reason. It goes against the universe to have more than one. I think the statue is the old man."

"What do the plaques with symbols mean, then?" Frank knelt down to inspect one closer.

Mira jumped the six feet down from the statue's kneecap to join him. "Each one's for a different gift. Here." She closed her eyes and put her hand on the symbol Frank was looking at, two dots that looked as if they were rotating around each other. "Hmm . . . this one's for telekinesis, the gift of moving things with your mind. See how they're going around in a circle?"

"Wait, you're a psychic!" Jon said, surprised.

"Well, at least, I'm learning about being one." Mira smiled. "We really aren't supposed to use our gifts without teachers around, but I do it sometimes. Especially if I'm here. No one ever comes here."

"Aren't you worried you'll get in trouble?" Frank asked.

"No. How can they be mad at me for practicing? I never understood that rule."

"Well, Miss Goody Two-Shoes, not so angelic after all." Jon smirked at her, and Mira sighed.

"I didn't say I always followed the rules, I just said it was my first time *in trouble*." She smirked back, and Frank could have sworn Jon almost bowed in honor of her. "I spend too much time around here. My dad is on the school board, and when you're asked to just hang around while he's in meetings all day and there are no kids to play with . . ."

"You entertain yourself," Frank finished, still studying the plaque. "Is it possible? I mean, to learn more than one gift?"

"I don't think so. It's just a story." Mira walked to another circle on the ground, which depicted what looked like an eye. "This one is for foresight—your gift, Jon. That one is telepathy, then empathy, sagacity, and clairvoyance."

"What about this one?" Jon asked.

Frank walked over to see the plaque Jon was peering at, but it was just a blank metal circle.

"Hmmm . . ." Mira knelt and put both her hands on it. "Ouch!" She pulled away as if it had burned her. "I don't know what that one is, but I know it doesn't want to tell me." She shook her head but then grinned. "Want to climb on his hands? It's super fun!"

Though still a little curious about the blank plaque, Frank quickly forgot about it as Jon and Mira raced to climb the statue.

They spent the next hour jumping, chasing, and clambering on and around the sculpture, Jon and Frank teaching Mira how to play hot lava. Eventually, worn out, they decided to start the trek home to change for dinner. Before they left, Mira made them both pinky swear they wouldn't tell anyone about the secret valley.

When time for dinner came around, she sat at Jon and Frank's table.

Mr. McClery

CHAPTER 12

Mrs. Sniffens wasn't all that bad; her bark was worse than her bite. It was a daily ritual for her to walk into the kitchen and turn on what she called the "golden oldies." She played songs from Elvis to the Temptations, and she loved to dance while she cooked. She was also gifted with telekinesis and constantly moved bags of food around and pulled pots and pans from across the room to speed up her process. Jon, Frank, and Mira helped mostly with peeling vegetables, chopping things, cleaning tables, and washing dishes.

Even though it was a lot of hard work, they made the best of it. Plus, it gave Jon and his brother a chance to get to know Mira better.

"My favorite thing about fall is the rain!" she said. "I grew up in the rain here. I love getting my boots out and sloshing through the big puddles. I'm not afraid to get dirty."

"Could have fooled me." Jon smirked at her, and she sloshed soapy water at him from the sink.

Classes went on as usual. On Monday, English had a small quiz, and they played dodgeball in PE. Jon ended up being on the same team as Damien and Mira, whereas Frank was on the opposite team. Jon usually got to the ball first because he was fast, but—remembering his promise to Mira—he only took a couple shots himself and was careful not to hog the ball, giving it away to other kids most of the time.

In the corner of his vision, Jon saw McClery, the General, standing at the gym side door, leaning against the frame and watching him.

"He sure keeps an eye on you," Frank commented. Jon didn't respond, focusing on the game instead.

After PE, Frank and Jon parted ways for their gift lessons. Jon walked down the windy path to the little cottage, took in a long breath, and opened the door, bracing himself for whatever McClery would toss his way today.

"Sir, I'm here!" He closed the door behind him and tossed his backpack on the floor.

The house was quiet; no one responded to Jon's shout. He heard a murmur in the study and headed that way.

"Sir?" he said again, slowly pushing open the slightly ajar door. The General was sitting in a high-backed leather chair facing a window that overlooked the forest. His cane was leaning against the chair arm.

"Go home, Jonny," he said quietly. It was the first time McClery had called him by any nickname. Jon couldn't see his face, but his tone didn't sound angry; if anything, he sounded distressed. "I can't teach you today."

"Sir, are you OK?" Jon asked.

"Just go!" The General raised his voice, and Jon quickly scooted out, grabbing his backpack and almost tripping on his way out the door.

What had just happened? What could possibly be wrong with McClery?

McClery went back to his same old self in the following days, telling Jon to wipe down the fridge, unpack books in the study, and even clean all the kitchen cupboards. This time, though, McClery didn't check his work.

The small amount of trust surprisingly pleased Jon. In some ways, Jon was proud of himself; he was becoming a pretty good worker. Between his "studies" with McClery and his detention with Mrs. Sniffens, all the manual labor was beginning to show in his arms. They were getting larger and more muscular. Jon couldn't help bragging and flexing for Damien and Nate.

Thursday during PE, Jon had another episode—shadows or phantoms or ghost figures, he wasn't sure what to call them. This time, they appeared as he was running down the field. A shadow of his brother was waving down the line, and a shadow of himself was running with the ball. Shadow Jon passed to shadow Frank, who shot at the goal for a score.

The thought made Jon smile. While Professor Yang didn't keep score, all the other kids did, and they were tied with blue. One more goal would put them ahead.

A minute later, Jon had the ball in his possession. He was heading up the field toward the opposing team goal when he heard a voice from the side.

"Pass here!" Frank called, waving. Jon kicked to him, and just as in his vision, Frank shot the ball straight past the keeper and into the goal. Jon cheered and ran to give his brother a hug.

"You passed to me! You never pass to me!" Frank said, shocked.

Jon laughed. "Because I knew you'd get it in, Franky," he said truthfully. Over his brother's shoulder, Jon spotted McClery once again standing on the sidelines, watching him. The man's eyes squinted; then he slowly turned and walked away.

Jon swallowed. Did he know?

That afternoon, Jon entered the cottage for gifts class with trepidation. He was sure McClery was going to give him another long list of chores, but as Jon walked in, something felt different.

McClery greeted him in a low voice from a chair by the fireplace. "Well, my boy, you've been doing good work. Have a seat!" He pointed to the tall lounge chair across from him.

Confused, Jon slowly moved to sit. "What work, sir?"

"Well, look around." He waved a hand about the room. It was, in fact, very different from the first time Jon had seen it. The dust and cobwebs were gone, replaced by a warm coziness. Pictures hung on the walls, the fireplace beside them heated the room, and the chairs they were sitting on had clean pillows. It was almost like a home now, instead of an abandoned cottage.

The photos on the wall showed a lush green countryside. McClery noticed Jon peering at them.

"My hometown in Ireland." He reclined back in his chair.

"Ireland? It's beautiful."

"Thank you. All right, Jonny, you ready for today's lesson?"

"Yes, sir."

"I would have us work on a gifts exercise today, but, well, you haven't had any more incidents." McClery sighed and shrugged. "I guess we can start to work on the yard . . ."

"Wait!" Jon stopped him, scooting to his chair's edge, excited by the prospect of actually learning something. "I, um . . . I may have had a couple."

McClery smirked knowingly and pulled a pen and paper from the side table into his lap. "Really? Interesting. Well then, tell me what you've been seeing."

Jon blinked at him, taken aback. "It's only happened twice recently. The first time, I saw Mira bumping into me at the cafeteria. I was watching it so closely that when I turned around, I actually did bump into her."

"Hmm . . . interesting." McClery wrote down some notes. "Go on."

"The other was today. I saw in a vision that if I kicked the ball to Frank, he would kick it in the goal. It happened about a minute before I did kick the ball to him. I knew it was the right thing to do, because he would get our team a goal."

"Because you saw it that way," McClery commented, and Jon nodded. "What happened to you in both cases is very important, Jonny. It may not seem that way, but it is." McClery's voice got low; it made Jon sit up and listen. "In the cafeteria, you stopped to watch your vision, and because you did, you were distracted and caused that scene to come true." McClery pushed up with his cane and leaned against the fireplace mantel, studying the flames. "And today on the soccer field when you saw Frank score, you chose to pass the ball to him because of that vision. In both cases, you made those things happen. Does that make sense?"

"Isn't the future always going to happen no matter

what?" Jon asked. "How did I change it?"

"My boy, the future is so much more complicated than that." McClery sighed visibly. "But today, we start with the basics. Today you learn what type of gift you have."

"OK, sir."

"No, Jon." McClery fixed him with a piercing glare. "Now, in this room, when I am teaching you, you may call me Liam. You may call me sir when you leave. Understood?"

"Yes, sir . . . I mean, Liam."

"All right." McClery stepped close to Jon's chair and looked down at him, leaning over his cane. Jon swallowed. "The day you saw Frank sick, when you bumped into Miss Camacho, even when you passed the soccer ball to Frank— all these things are called flash precognitions. They last for a few seconds and will only show you a short distance into the future. Very useful in combat, but extremely illegal in gambling or playing sports." He smirked.

"Oh . . ." Jon's face turned red. "That's difficult to control."

"It always is," McClery said, a warning in his voice. "Jon, as an oracle, you may be able to see into people's futures. You may be able to prevent danger. You may be able to even calculate someone's death. But to use this gift unwisely can create worse terrors than you know."

"Liam, what other forms of foresight are there?"

McClery stepped away, back to the fireplace. "Several. For instance, stargazing, the ability to read the sky. Some see the future in sand, smoke, dust. Some can only predict the future by drawing or painting. There may be a time you'll be able to sense a future based on emotion, yours or others. But the strongest and rarest way to predict the future is through dreams. They are also the hardest to interpret." McClery eyed Jon and took in a deep breath. "Jon, you don't have dreams like that, do you?"

"I wouldn't know if I did, Liam. I'm still new to all this." Jon was relieved when McClery nodded his head.

"All right then, consider this the first day of your training."

"Training? What am I training for?" Jon asked, a bit nervously.

McClery chuckled. "Why, the future, of course."

The Sanctuary of Knowledge

CHAPTER 13

You really need to do this now? Jon said in his mind.

"Yes, Jon. I need to do this now," Frank answered out loud. Over the last four weeks, Frank's skill at reading one mind at a time had improved, but Jon's mind was still the easiest to read.

"It's probably because you two are twins. Twins share a bond that's found nowhere else in nature," Nate had commented one day as Frank was practicing.

As a challenge, however, Professor Owens had asked him to practice on different voices, not to stick with what was easy. So his friends had agreed to help him practice.

Jon, Mira, Nate, and Damien were bundled up in warm coats and hats and sitting on top of a school picnic table just outside Aries house. Frank stood facing them. As a Leo,

Mira wasn't allowed in Aries house, so they'd started meeting outside, even in the cold mid-November weather.

"All right, now, Mira, you think of something." Frank adjusted the notepaper he was using to write down what he heard from his friends' minds.

I'm going to climb that tree over there. She winked at him, and Frank nodded, writing down her thoughts. When he verified them with her, pride swelled in his chest.

"Now I'll ask a question, and I want you all to think about it. But I'm going to try and focus on one person's thoughts." Frank cleared his own mind and slowly tuned out the background noise. "OK, if you could be anywhere in the world, where would it be?"

China . . . With my mother—Space! The voices muddled together as he received them all at once. Closing his eyes, he listened for the loudest voice to pick out. *I would go to the river.* Frank opened his eyes and pointed at Jon. "The river?"

"Yep, you're doing good, Franky," Jon teased. "Are we almost done?"

"Yeah, I guess."

Even though it was chilly outside, they all decided to walk to the river. It was a couple miles from the school grounds, but with permission, students were allowed to take the trek through the forest.

It was too cold to swim or float, so they just hung out on

the driftwood that lined the riverbank.

"Yesterday, Professor Gonzales brought in an artifact from the Sanctuary of Knowledge for us to touch and examine," Mira said as she threw pebbles into the river's current.

"The Sanctuary of Knowledge? That sounds made up," Jon said from his perch atop a large boulder.

"No, it's true. I've heard of it too." Nate was examining a plant near the river. "Professor Wyatt says we get to go down there in a couple years to look at the library. He says they have the most sophisticated and complicated books he's ever read."

"Yeah, remember, Jon? Professor Mortensen mentioned it when we first got here. Said you can't go down there unless you have a teacher with you," Frank added.

Jon shrugged. "OK, Mira, what was this artifact?"

"It sounds silly, but it was a bowl."

"A bowl?" Damien rolled his eyes. "Did the president eat out of it or something?"

"No. It was found on an archeological dig in Egypt. It's over four thousand years old, which means it's full of life." Mira tossed another stone into the river, and it skipped twice. Earlier in the year, Mira had told Frank that many kids who studied clairvoyance ended up as archeologists or historians, learning about the past through the strong emotions held within particular objects. Others went into criminal justice and detective work.

"What happened?" Nate asked.

"Well, Sandy Henson heard a conversation in another language when she touched it. Professor Gonzalez said it sounded like ancient Egyptian. She recorded it and will let us know tomorrow. I only saw flashes of sand when it was my turn. We get to study it more tomorrow." Mira started climbing up the boulder the boys were sitting on.

"That sounds way more exciting than my class," Damien commented. "Professor Vidra just turned on some music and had us close our eyes while sitting on mats. Then we were told to hold hands with a classmate and sense what the music was doing to them. I don't think I'll ever get good at my gift, and if I do, what kinda job am I going to have?"

"My mom's a cop," Frank said, and Damien's eyes widened.

"Really?"

"Yep, and she does hostage negotiations. Her gift to feel people's problems and even calm them down helps her save lives," Jon added. "Maybe you can do something like that, Damien. Don't give up."

"Do you think empaths ever get to go down to the Sanctuary of Knowledge?" Damien asked as they headed back to the school.

"Not sure, buddy," Frank answered, putting an arm around him.

As Christmas break approached, teachers started preparing students for their end-of-term exams. Professor Owens assigned a five-page paper, Professor Wyatt started the practice papers for a cumulative math test, Professor Gonzalez paired her students for a lab project, and Professor Vidra assigned a group presentation on "gifted people and their contributions to society."

The only classes that didn't give them homework were their gifts courses and PE.

Jon was gaining plenty of insight from McClery now that he'd finally started teaching him about his gift. A couple weeks ago, Jon had realized that the cottage they met in was McClery's home at the school. The old man had used Jon's lessons as a way to clean up the building. Now that the General was spending quality time with him, however, the idea didn't upset him as much.

"Jonny, you keepin' that journal I gave ya?" McClery asked that Friday afternoon. Fridays were double periods of gifts class, after which students were released early for the weekend. It was almost everyone's favorite school day.

"Yeah, every time it happens, I write down how long it

happened for, what time of day, and what I was feeling—everything you wanted." Jon pulled out the journal and handed it to him.

McClery sat comfortably in his chair, a cup of coffee beside him. Leisurely, he turned the pages of Jon's book. "All right, Jonny boy, what was this that happened on the school trails?"

"Well, we were walking, and a shadow Mira tripped over a tree root and fell on her hands. So instead of letting it happen, I took her arm as we passed by the tree. She didn't fall like I'd seen."

"Hmm . . ." McClery raised an eyebrow. "And you feel like you changed this possible future?"

"Yes." Jon had thought a lot about this peculiar incident. It was the only time he'd ever stopped what happened in his visions.

"And how did that make you feel?"

"Good," Jon said, "really good. I saved her from getting hurt."

"Aww . . . so you've taken the first step into being an oracle. You said it made you feel good. Why is that?"

"Because I had control. I was able to change things."

"It felt good, Jonny, because you had power. Power to control *fate*—something everyone in your life said you couldn't change. Do you think that's true now?"

"It may be true for some people, but not me." Jon's eyes got wide as he thought about it. The idea of shifting the future, making a difference or a profit, was irresistible. "I can control fate . . ."

"The greatest lie that exists is the one we convince ourselves is the truth. Come with me, Jonny. I have something to show you." McClery rose from his chair with care, gripping his cane, and headed toward the cottage door. Jon followed him out the door and along a trail into the woods.

It didn't take long before they'd reached an old cement bunker, partially buried. An electric lantern hung on a rusted nail under the overhanging entrance. McClery pointed for Jon to grab it.

"Where are we?" Jon asked.

"The Sanctuary of Knowledge." McClery pulled out an old key with a medallion keychain attached; it resembled the school emblem. He shoved the key into the door's keyhole. "Give me a hand, boy."

Jon helped move the heavy metal door, then looked into the pitch blackness beyond while McClery grabbed the lantern and beckoned him forward. When the squeaking metal door closed behind them, it latched with a shattering *thud*.

It felt as if the fall breeze had been sucked out of the

dark hall, leaving a lifeless vacuum. The remaining air tasted stale and musty, as if they'd been locked inside a casket. The lantern illuminated a cement-walled hallway, the ground nothing more than dirt-crusted concrete. As they traveled farther into the bunker, it got colder. Jon wished he'd brought a second jacket.

"Turn to your left down there," McClery instructed.

The turn led them to another metal door, this one engraved with an eye symbol on it. Pulling out the key again, McClery unlocked the door and pushed it open. "Security is tight here. In order to visit the sanctuary, teachers must sign out this key." He shook it in front of Jon with a smirk and then stepped into the room. Jon instantly felt warmer as he entered. The floor and walls had to be insulated.

McClery reached past him to flip a switch on the wall. A single bulb hanging from the ceiling flickered to life, and Jon gasped.

Hanging on the walls were decorative tapestries, paintings, and drawings of cities—some in flames, others crumbling. Framed star charts with lines of equations under them leaned against chairs and tables. A large shelf in the back was packed with loose papers squished between ancient-looking books. The thing that drew Jon's attention the most was a tarnished silver statue of a guard, no more than twelve inches tall.

McClery stepped forward, giving Jon a better view. "This is the room of known oracle knowledge."

"The paintings?"

"Disasters. This one is the 1908 San Francisco fire"—McClery pointed to the title at the bottom—"predicted thirteen years before it happened, and this one is the Great Seattle Fire of 1889, predicted five years before it happened."

But Jon was drawn to another painting. It was a drawing of two towers, one engulfed in smoke. The title at the bottom read "September 11, 2001, predicted on February 4, 1965." The initials N. S. were scrawled beside the dates. Jon had heard about the tragic event in school. The image was very similar to one his teacher had shown the class.

"Someone knew about September eleventh thirty-six years before it happened?"

"Yes," McClery said sadly.

Jon turned to study his teacher. "Who is N. S.?"

"The person who predicted it. No one you know." The man's tone discouraged Jon from asking again. "Only the most accurate and detailed predictions are kept here. The rest are scanned into a computer for records. These star charts also predict big events, as well as these ancient tapestries. There are some predictions here that haven't even happened yet."

Jon took the room in slowly. It was the first time he'd seen anything from other oracles. Somehow, it made him feel less like a rarity. There had been others like him; perhaps they were still around.

"What I really wanted to show you, Jonny." McClery pointed to the tarnished statue, a guard with a helmet and sword. It sat on a pedestal draped in a velvety cloth, its small carved hands holding a translucent ball. Jon stood in front of it to get a better look. "Energy is a very powerful thing. Life-force energy is the strongest. You'll find many objects like this in our world. This one has been used by oracles in training for over a thousand years. The school is now its permanent home." Leaning down, McClery whispered into Jon's ear, "Go ahead and touch it, but be gentle."

Swallowing, Jon very lightly brushed his fingers across the statue's helmet.

A rush swarmed his head, and for a moment, Jon felt as if his brain were on fire. His vision darkened, then quickly filled with images—images of swirling stars and fog. From the fog came whispers, distinct voices, hundreds of them, each saying something different. Some voices talked about wars, others about famine, some about hope; there were so many.

Jon remembered something Frank had told him about telepathy. If he focused carefully on the strongest voice, that voice would get stronger and eventually overpower the others. Jon tried, and soon a female voice sung through the murky cloud of noise.

"I saw him. He was sitting in a place of power, like a room or something. In his hand, he held a knife and was looking over the body of a woman dressed in red."

Jon could see it, a man with long dark hair, ruffled as if he'd been in a struggle. He was wearing a tuxedo, his bow tie undone, and a bloody handprint stained his button-up shirt. Below him was the red dress, but the woman's face was a blur. The man was pacing.

"I don't know his name or where he is or who he killed. I just know it will happen. Someone must do something . . ."

Jon peeled his fingers away from the wretched statue. His face was moist with sweat, his breath short and hurried. He stared at his hands, which were shaking slightly. "What happened?"

"What do you mean, boy?" McClery asked with a smirk.

"The man. He killed someone. I don't know who. The woman who saw it, she didn't know either. Was he ever caught?"

"Jonny, what you experienced were the voices of predictions that have yet to come true. Who's to say they will even come true in our lifetime?" McClery gestured toward the paintings. "Sometimes we see the future and there's nothing we can do to stop it from coming true. How can one person prevent an earthquake or a fire, or a plane from crashing into a building thirty-six years in the future?"

"I don't get it, Liam. If what I have doesn't help anyone, why do they call it gift?"

"Jonny, I never said it was a gift."

Something heavy sunk in Jon's stomach. "I can't control fate?" he asked sadly.

"Controlling fate is a power you do not want, Jonny. In the end, fate will always end up controlling you. It controls us all. That's the balance of this life." McClery nodded to the statue. "We call it the Guardian of Whispers. We keep all predictions in the computer now, but this artifact is useful for training new oracles. I trained on it. All the great oracles have a prediction in there. Who knows? Maybe one day you'll have one of your prophecies in there as well."

"Do you?"

"No." McClery stared scornfully at the guardian. "I'm not a great oracle, Jonny. I'm not even a great man."

Jon let the silence linger between them. He wasn't sure what to say. His experience with the guardian had left his mind whirling and his body drained.

"Let's take ya back," McClery said at last. Slowly they stood, turned off the light, and closed the door behind them.

∩∩

With exams finally over, teachers were more willy-nilly about homework and assignments. Not that Frank minded.

Spending time with his family would be easier if he didn't have to study.

Frank's last telepathy class was on the coldest day of the year. The school's heating system was having a hard time keeping up with the freezing weather. No matter how many socks and layers of clothes Frank put on, he couldn't get warm enough. Traveling from one building to the next was torture, and he'd finally experienced what everyone called "freezing fog."

Mira, Jon, and Frank's Saturday tradition was to head up to the secret hideout. This last Saturday, however, had been too cold, so instead, they'd decided to play board games in the cafeteria after lunch. Mrs. Sniffens had put some hot cocoa and Christmas treats out for everyone.

Mrs. Sniffens had grown quite fond of them during their detention duty, and they of her. She often left a few extra desserts for them on the counter after dinner or lunch, and Jon, Mira, and Frank would still help prep breakfast on Saturday evenings so the kitchen staff could get an extra hour of sleep on Sunday. Helping out also had its benefits; walking home afterward was the only time they could be out after curfew.

Nighttime had been beautiful recently. Carver had been right—it did rain a lot in Washington—but what Carver didn't know was when Washington got its coldest, there wasn't a cloud in the sky. It had been sunny all week, and the nights were starry. On the school trails—without street lamps—the sky looked as if it were lit by a million candles. There was also many shooting stars. Mira, Jon, and Frank had taken to lying on the chilly grass and counting the meteors as they flew by.

Curfew was always in effect, but Washington in the winter got dark early. At four o'clock, right as class was getting out, the stars would begin appearing.

Frank looked out the window in his classroom and saw frozen grass—not snow, *frozen grass*. Carver would never believe him. Everything was frozen. It looked as if someone had drained all the color out of a photograph, except for the ice shimmering like glitter in the sun. The window itself boasted an amazing artwork of crystallization around the frame.

Frost was very pretty but very cold. Sitting by the window had its drawbacks.

"All right class," Professor Owens calmly greeted them as they paired up, "as this is our last class, I want to send out one more warning." He glared over his mustache. "Younger students especially, you must try not to use your gifts at home. Here you are protected by your teachers, by our collective minds. Back home you may experience hearing more voices. They may be louder, more concentrated and frequent. Remember, younger students, that you are still on basic levels. You are practicing reading minds, being able to distinguish voices, narrowing in on others' thoughts. At the end of spring term, you will be tested on these skills before you can advance to basic level two next year."

Paige raised her hand. "Sir, what is basic level two?"

"Excellent question. In level two we will learn the ability to relay information to others through telepathy, to share a conversation through telepathy, and distance telepathy—being able to send a message to someone in another room, for example." Owens turned and started writing their new exercise on the board.

The assignment was easy enough. They were to do what Professor Owens called "blinders," where you watched a person in the room and read their thoughts without them knowing. The only complicated part was keeping your own thoughts clear. With break so soon, Frank couldn't help letting his mind wander to his family.

In fact, only one kid in the room *wasn't* thinking about his family or the upcoming break. The boy was sitting off in the corner, his shoulders slumped. He was in the same grade as Frank but about half his size. Frank couldn't stop watching him, his concern growing.

After class, Frank approached Professor Owens's desk. "Sir, the small boy who sits in the back there . . ."

"Braydon? What about him? Was he cheating?" Professor Owens grumbled as he stacked assignments the class had turned in.

"Um . . . no, sir. I don't think he has anywhere to go home to, or he doesn't want to go home. I read from him that he wasn't sure what he was doing after term. I just think someone should check on him. You know, like a teacher."

Owens stared at Frank with a quirked brow for a moment, then his face seemed to soften. "How perceptive of you, Franklin. Don't worry, I'll see to it."

Satisfied, Frank smiled and nodded. "Have a nice Christmas, Professor Owens." He waved, and Professor Owens awkwardly waved back.

A Holiday Trip

CHAPTER 14

"Well, there you go, Pete. I told you they'd be back in no time at all. It's almost like they never left," Eugene commented.

Jon sighed in relief as he dropped his backpack on the floor. Frank dropped his bag on top of his brother's, quickly stuffing the stardust stone back into his shirt when it slipped out; Professor Mortensen had given it back to him for their holiday break.

"Oh, Genie missed us . . ." Jon smirked.

"You're home! You're home!" Peter spouted out, his words coming a mile a minute. "You know, while you were gone, I made a friend! A real friend! His name is Simon, and he likes books just as much as I do, and sometimes he comes over . . ."

Everyone shared hugs. Aunt Gladys's were so tight Jon

felt as if his eyeballs might pop out. Clara hugged them hard around the belly, clinging to Jon long enough that he had to walk forward with her still attached.

Even though it had only been a couple of months, it felt like ages since they'd left Florida, and Jon wasn't sure he liked that feeling. It was nice to hear Peter talk about simple things, to be reminded that people lived uncomplicated lives outside of West Hills school.

"You know, Peter," Frank said, "at our school there's a huge library. Some students get to sit and study the books all day. We even have a new friend who can read a book and remember almost everything in it. You'd love it!"

Peter's eyes went wide. "Wow, that sounds amazing!"

Christmas break started out wonderful, although finding a real Christmas tree—like the evergreens that littered Washington—was not only expensive but nearly impossible. One of the many Reed family holiday traditions was to put up an eight-foot artificial tree and decorate it all together.

Gathered in the living room, listening to the sounds of Bing Crosby singing, "I'm Dreaming of a White Christmas," each was tasked with a different part of tree setup. Eugene and Dad untangled and fixed strings of lights as the twins sorted out the Christmas ornaments.

Their parents had grilled them on how school was going as soon as they'd gotten home. Jon had told them about their new friends but not about the trouble they landed in for the food fight. His parents had already thoroughly lectured him on the topic by phone.

"We get to play soccer!" Frank had told them, to the amusement of both parents.

Dad had been particularly interested in Jon's gifts teacher.

"He's all right," Jon said, not really wanting to give specifics. "Mr. McClery knows a lot about telling the future. We get along OK." It was vague, but it was all Jon felt like sharing. In truth, he wasn't sure how he felt about McClery yet.

Organizing the glass ornaments was an easy and enjoyable task, one of Jon's favorite things to do. As he stood up to get another box, Mom set a humming Clara down by the tree with a silver ribbon to untangle. Peter was on a tall stepladder above his little sister, puffing out the fake tree branches so they appeared more realistic.

As his hands landed on the next box of ornaments, a sudden wave hit Jon's head, and his stomach did a backflip. The room was spinning. Jon pressed one hand to his temple and the other to his tummy.

Then it happened.

Shadow people again—one shadow of Peter on the ladder, reaching. Shadow Peter's head turned, and the ladder tipped, sending him straight into the tree. Trying to avoid a disaster, shadow Peter gripped the bannister behind him to stop his fall, but it was too late for the shadow tree. It fell directly onto a small shadow Clara below.

"N . . . no!" Jon stuttered loudly.

Surprised by his outburst, Peter tipped and lost his footing on the ladder. Jon knew what was about to happen. His feet released from what felt like cement, and he grabbed Clara's hand, barely pulling her out from under the falling tree.

Clara shouted, and the whole family stood in alarm. At the sight of the fallen tree, an unstable Peter, a crying Clara, and Jon's panicked breathing, Mom ran to Jon's side.

"What just happened?" Eugene's eyes were wide, his hand still holding a strand of lights.

"I'm sorry." Peter looked down at the tree, tears in his eyes. "Jon scared me."

Feeling dazed, Jon couldn't open his mouth to say anything.

"Jonathan, are you OK?" Dad asked.

Jon could barely shake his head. What had he seen? Was he the cause? The room was silent, everyone waiting for his response.

"I'm sorry. I'm sorry, everyone. It's just . . . I saw . . ." Jon couldn't finish; it sounded so foolish. He wished McClery were there to walk him through what had happened, to help him process. But he wasn't. Jon was alone.

Taking the silence as a chance to escape, Jon ran up to his room, closing the door behind him.

∽⌒

"Give him some time, Franklin," Mom whispered into his ear, putting a hand on his shoulder to stop him from following his brother upstairs.

He nodded and took her advice, waiting till just before dinner to sneak into their bedroom to talk.

"Hey," he said. Jon was lying on the lower bunk, staring at the bunk above him. "You hungry? Dinner is ready. Aunt Gladys made your favorite, homemade pizza. You know, the one with the white sauce and the artichoke hearts and—"

"Not hungry," Jon said sullenly.

"There's also sundried tomatoes and olives—"

"I said I'm not hungry," Jon said sternly, turning away.

Frank took a deep breath and let it out through his nose. It took everything in him not to read his brother's thoughts, but he could make a pretty good guess.

After a short silence, Frank glanced over at Jon and sighed. "You saw it happen, didn't you?"

"Yeah," Jon replied after a minute. "I made it happen."

"How so?" Frank asked, but Jon just shrugged. "Professor Owens says it's normal for our abilities to be stronger and more frequent now that we're practicing more."

"Hmmm . . ." Jon answered disinterestedly.

"In fact, earlier, I know I'm not supposed to, but I read Eugene's mind," Frank said slyly.

"Was it empty?" They both laughed.

"No, but he does miss us. He said, 'It's good to have those weirdoes back.'" That got another chuckle out of his brother. "Come on, get something to eat."

After another minute, Jon sighed and nodded, and they both went downstairs for food.

By the time Christmas day came around, the incident with Jon had been totally forgotten. Peter woke up earliest, rousing Frank and his other siblings in his excitement. Every Christmas, the kids had to suffer the torture of staring at the piles of presents under the tree and not being allowed to open them. It was a rule; they had to wait until their parents were up, and they had to finish Christmas breakfast first.

"Aunt Gladys, you've outdone yourself this year!" Eugene cried while devouring a huge cinnamon roll. Frank couldn't help but agree; his tower of bacon was dripping with maple syrup.

"It's an all-night adventure to feed this family." Aunt Gladys smiled and kissed the top of Eugene's head. "But it's a pleasure, darling."

They always stayed in their pajamas all day on Christmas, and because of that, Frank always forgot to brush his teeth. Not that he cared much. There was too many family memories to be made.

When he opened his gifts, Frank was ecstatic to see new comic books, a whole new set of drawing pencils, and a sketch book. Eugene got a small build-your-own-robot kit and a new bike helmet. Peter, of course, got more books and a large beanbag chair to read them in. Clara was just happy to have roller skates and some building blocks. She loved to build things, especially with Eugene.

Jon was the last to open his presents. He got some spy goggles, which he loved. Then he opened a smaller box and pulled out a new Han Solo action figure.

"How did you know I lost it?" Jon asked, surprised.

Mom smiled. "Frank wrote and told us."

"Yeah, unlike some of us, I wrote Mom and Dad every couple weeks," Frank teased.

Jon looked down, embarrassed. "Oops . . . sorry."

Both their parents laughed.

∼⌒

Silence, complete and deafening silence, as if everything had been sucked from the atmosphere. Then, slowly, with a tapping of crickets, the sound of a marsh.

Open your eyes, Jon told himself.

He was alone. Fog pooled around his ankles, so thick

he couldn't see the ground, thick and gray. Jon shivered, murmured voices tickling his ear. His hands were damp and chilled from the mist, and he rubbed them together, then tucked them under his armpits for warmth.

He wanted to walk—look for someplace to get warm—but it was impossible; his boots were stuck in the mud, sinking into the mushy swamp below. The murmuring was getting louder, but Jon still couldn't make out the words. Everything sounded muffled, as if he were underwater.

The fog rolled back from the horizon a little, and he caught the faint outline of trees or figures in the distance. A figure to his right was moving closer.

"Where's your coat?" the figure asked. As it approached, he saw it was Frank.

"What?" Jon asked, his teeth chattering. The voice, his brother's voice, was now crystal clear, as though he were whispering into his ear.

"Come on, let's go." Frank waved and started walking off.

"Frank, I can't! I'm stuck." Jon panicked, but his brother stopped and turned back to him.

Fear transformed Frank's features as he stared at something above Jon's head. "Jon! Behind you!"

It was the figures again, but not trees. They were *shadows*—moving shaking, rushing—massive shadows consuming the mist and crawling toward them. Jon leaned forward and tried to pull his foot out of his boot without success. It felt glued in. Then he started sinking, deeper and deeper, at an alarming rate.

"Frank! Help me! Grab my hand!" Jon reached out, but the mud hole was eating him up. Frank shook his head and then, with what looked like regret and shame, turned and ran away.

Jon was up to his neck in mud, but before it sucked him completely under, a strong hand gripped his shirt and pulled him free.

Then the same hand wrapped around his neck.

Jon scrabbled at his attacker's arm, trying desperately to break away, but he was too weak. The voices were back—crying, murmuring, almost pleading—but he couldn't tell where they were coming from. It was as if they were in his head. Soon, black tunnels appeared in his vision, and he heard the frantic beat of his heart, as if it were trying to escape his chest.

With the last of his energy, he tried to yell. The word tore from his mouth as blackness overtook him.

"*No!*"

"Wake up . . . please, Jon, wake up . . ."

Hands were grabbing at his clothes. Jon's eyes flew open, and his mind was assaulted with the bright overhead light of his bedroom and the tear-filled eyes of his father looking down at him. Dad was clutching Jon's pajamas with shaking hands.

"Oh gosh . . . Thank you, Lord," Dad said before pulling Jon tightly into his arms. Confused and still getting his bearings, he saw Mom standing in the doorway, one hand grasping at her heart, her cellphone at her ear.

"He's back," she whispered into the phone.

Frank was standing beside her, his hair a mess and his eyes wide. Peter was crying quietly on his own bed, his knees pulled to his chest.

"It's OK," Jon said, realizing with relief that it had all been just a terrifying dream. "I'm OK. It was only a nightmare."

"Nightmare? Jon, we've been trying to wake you for five minutes," Frank squeaked.

"No, Dr. Harrison, he seems OK now," Mom said into her phone as she moved into the hallway.

"Jon, what were you dreaming about?" Dad asked, catching his breath, his hands still firmly on Jon's forearms.

"Yeah, you were yelling . . ." Peter said quietly.

"I . . ." Jon looked around at all the faces, suddenly uncomfortable. "I don't remember . . ." It was a lie, but he didn't want to worry his family. The only person Jon really wanted to talk to was McClery. When had he started trusting the man?

Dad ran a trembling hand through his hair and then

down his face. "You sure know how to stay the center of attention, Jonathan."

Once everyone was satisfied with his mental state, they returned to their beds. Jon lay awake until he knew his brothers were asleep, then reached into his backpack, pulled out his journal, and wrote down all the details from the dream he could remember. He wanted to be ready for his next session with McClery.

The rest of their holiday break was uneventful and pleasant, but when the time came to say goodbye, it was even harder for Jon than it had been the first time. He wouldn't see his family until summer break, at least five months. He promised his parents he would write more.

It didn't take long after liftoff for the twins to fall asleep. This time, Han Solo stayed safely in Jon's backpack.

An Actual Fight

CHAPTER 15

Frank unpacked his backpack and enjoyed the peace of his room before his roommates or Jon could disturb it. It had been a good break—no homework, family time, presents—but he couldn't shake his worry for Jon.

Even though Frank didn't want to admit it out loud, he looked up to his smart, adventurous brother a great deal. It was easy to let him take charge. Even if he didn't always agree, it was hard to say no to Jon.

That was why seeing him closed off felt so strange. When Jon had started yelling in his sleep—thrashing, screaming, and shouting Frank's name—Frank had run to get their parents. He'd felt totally helpless when they hadn't been able to wake him. Was that what it was like for Jon when Frank had his episodes?

Since then, though, Jon had seemed like himself. Well, mostly. There were times Frank could swear his brother was hiding something, and he didn't like it. They usually shared everything.

"Your brother is still drooling over the tryouts poster." Damien laughed as he walked into their room and threw his bag on his bed.

Frank rolled his eyes. "Doesn't surprise me."

∽⏐⏑

The first thing Jon did at his next gift's class was share his episode and dream with McClery. From one of the high-back lounge chairs by the fireplace, Jon watched McClery read and reread his journal notes, his hand clamped over his chin in concentration. Occasionally his teacher would grunt or murmur as Jon waited patiently for an answer.

"OK, Jonny," McClery said at last, "let's talk about your episode first. What do you think about it?"

"I caused it." Jon looked down at his hands.

"Hmm . . . *caused it*. I think it's funny you use those words. That isn't what you said when you made your vision happen at PE."

"Yes, but that was different. I saw a good thing and made it come true. This time, I responded to my vision and caused a bad thing to happen. I could have killed Clara." Jon's chest ached just thinking about it.

"But you didn't. I would go so far as to say while, yes, you may have started the events but the outcome was very different—which, I would also say, is because of you." McClery sat back to study him, and Jon rubbed the back of his head.

"I guess so, Liam, I'm just so confused by all this stuff."

"It's probability, boy. This episode is a great example of how time and probability are fluid. You see things—things that may be caused by you or not. In the end, it wasn't as you saw it because you saw it in advance."

Jon just shook his head, and McClery sighed.

"There is still much to learn. Now, about your dream . . ." He cleared his throat and leaned forward. "Have you had this dream before?"

"Well . . ." Jon thought back. "I think I may have once or twice. But it changes a little . . ."

"What kind of changes?"

"Well, I don't remember feeling cold in the ones before. That was new. It's like my senses are stronger each time I have it."

McClery's expression became guarded, and he paused long enough to make Jon uncomfortable. "No," he whispered with a wave of his hand, "too young."

"Sir?"

"What? Oh, yes." McClery refocused on him. "I don't think you should be concerned about these dreams. Kids have nightmares, many recurring. It's unlikely it's related to your ability." He looked at the clock. "Lessons are done today."

Jon stood to leave, but as he made his way to the door, McClery stopped him.

"Jon, if you do have another of these dreams, write it down. No harm in keeping things documented."

∩⌒

Three weeks into school the days started to warm up a bit, but that didn't stop the most recognizable weather in the Pacific Northwest: *rain*. A chill wind picked up raindrops and blew them on students' faces as they walked to and from class. Miserable, Frank wrapped his school jacket collar around his nose and cheeks for protection.

He'd gotten out of class early and was on his way back to Aries house for a small nap, but the sound of raised voices behind Libra house stopped him. Rounding the corner to see what was going on, he caught sight of Mira's dark wavy hair. A stocky older kid was standing over her, glaring, his fists clenched at his sides.

Frank didn't know the boy's name, but he recognized him from Scorpio house. Mira's house, Leo, and Scorpio were known rivals.

"So, you think you're better than us all," the stocky kid said. "It must be nice getting whatever you want handed to you on a silver platter." The boy towered over Mira, but she held her ground, glaring back with her arms crossed.

"Hey, is everything OK?" Frank interrupted, and Mira looked over at him. Her face was scrunched up in anger, but he knew she wasn't mad at him.

"Yeah, we were just finished here," she said, her voice tight.

"I don't think so, missy." The older boy stepped closer. "You get whatever you want because your dad is on the school board. Some of us actually have to work hard." He was nearly nose-to-nose with Mira. Frank took a step forward protectively, but Mira stopped him with a warning glance.

"I don't know what you're talking about, Syrus. Is this about what Mrs. Gonzalez said? If you're worried about favoritism, you should go talk to her." Mira tried to move around him only to be blocked.

"Where do you think you're going?" Syrus growled, grabbing her arm.

"Hey! Let me go."

Frank couldn't stop himself; his body went into autopilot. He yanked Syrus's shoulder back so the boy was facing him instead of Mira. "Keep your hands off her!"

"Frank, no!" Mira said sharply.

Syrus was now sneering, red-faced, at Frank. He looked like a kettle ready to boil over. "Who do you think you are?" The bigger boy grabbed Frank's jacket and pulled him off the ground. *Stupid redhead kid, I'll give you something be upset about. Stay out of my way.*

Frank's adrenaline and fear made reading Syrus's mind easy, and he gulped.

The boy's fist flung forward hitting Frank's cheek. Frank dropped to the grass and covered his face with his hands, expecting another round of abuse. Mira was yelling at Syrus, but Frank didn't open his eyes, afraid of being greeted by white knuckles.

But then Syrus grunted in surprise, giving Frank the courage to peek.

A redhaired blur had grabbed Syrus's coat. With his hand still frozen in a raised fist, Syrus was flung around and punched square in the face by Jon.

"That's my brother!" Jon shouted as he tackled the boy to the ground. Frank sat up, dazed and stunned, and watched Jon pin Syrus to the ground with his legs and hit him over and over. Syrus fought back, pulling Jon's hair as they rolled around in the grass.

"Stop!" Mira tried to pull Jon away, but he just shrugged

her off.

"Stop is right!" Another louder voice said.

Frank glanced up to see a small crowd had formed around them, and towering over everyone was Superintendent Mortensen.

"Professor Mortensen, help, please!" Syrus cried. Jon was now sitting on top of him.

Mortensen grabbed Jon by the back of his shirt. "That is enough!"

Reluctantly, Jon removed himself from Syrus, but his hands remained clenched in fists, and he continued to glare.

"Now," Mortensen huffed, "what is going on here?"

"He just attacked me for no reason!" Still on the ground, Syrus held his bloody nose and pointed at Jon, then he also pointed at Frank. "That one too. Just attacked me!"

"That's not true!" said Mira, her eyes watery and her face red. "Syrus grabbed my arm, and they were trying to stop it."

"Boys, is this true?" Mortensen's hand still gripped Jon's arm.

"Frank didn't do anything," Jon said with a heavy breath. "If anyone should be in trouble for fighting, it's me and him." He pointed at Syrus.

"We'll see who's at fault when I'm done talking to all of you. Syrus, go to the medical center and get cleaned up, and then I want to see you in my office. Mira and Franklin, you both go there now. I want to have a word with Jonathan here." Mortensen's tone gave no room for argument, and Frank got up, his stomach twisting.

"Come on, Franklin." Mira reached for his hand, and they started walking back to school together. "Thank you for trying to stop Syrus, but you didn't need to do anything. I could have handled it."

"I know." Frank half smiled in embarrassment. "You're the strongest girl I know."

"What is that supposed to mean?" She gave him a teasing glare, and Frank blushed.

"I mean—" he started, but she put up a hand.

"I know what you mean. Look, you think Jon is in big trouble?"

Frank just shook his head. "If he is, it wouldn't be the first time. He gets crazy if he thinks I'm being bullied. Once I was being teased by one of Eugene's friends, and Jon tackled the kid, then told him he was ugly and no one liked him. He made him cry. We were only six at the time." Frank sighed. "What was going on with you and Syrus anyway?"

"I don't really know him well at all. He's in my class with Professor Gonzalez. I think he was upset because today Gonzalez used me as an example for the class, and everyone took notes on what I was saying. But I earned it! I was getting the best images and sounds from the Egyptian artifact." Sighing, she wiped the rain from her face. "I think he was jealous."

"So, your dad really is on the school board?" Frank smirked, but Mira's returning glare made him put his hands up. "OK, sorry."

"It's just . . . I don't like people to know. They get all weird around me, like Syrus did." Mira made a face and sat on the bench outside of Mortensen's door. Frank sat down beside her, not sure how to comfort his friend.

Several minutes went by, but it felt like an eternity to Frank. He unconsciously rubbed at his sore cheek—Syrus had hit hard—but his real concern was Jon. What was taking so long?

No sooner had he asked himself that than Jon appeared with Mortensen. Frank opened his mouth to speak but was silenced by the authoritative voice of their superintendent.

"All right, we will start with you, Franklin."

Frank stood to follow Mortensen into his office.

Tryouts

CHAPTER 16

Jon slumped into the seat next to Mira. He exhaled and tried to relax, leaning his head against the wall and closing his eyes.

"What happened?" Mira asked.

"Violence won't be tolerated." Jon smirked, repeating Mortensen's words. "I have detention for the next month. Strike two . . ."

"Well, you shouldn't have fought Syrus. There are other ways to fight without using your fists."

"He hit Frank." Jon's temper bubbled up again at the memory. His rage-fueled response had been automatic. Nothing could have stopped it. "I couldn't let him get away with that."

"I still disagree. It's nice how loyal you are to your brother, but you must control yourself. How did you know what was going on, anyway?"

"That's the weird thing. I didn't know. I was walking back from my lesson with Professor McClery, and I knew Frank was in trouble. Like he was crying for help." Jon shrugged. "Must be a twin thing."

"Maybe . . ." Mira said slowly, as if uncertain, but Jon didn't press.

When all was said and done, everyone was sent back to their houses. Syrus and Jon had detention for a month, and Frank and Mira were given a lecture about how to handle bullies in the future. Jon's parents were also being sent a notice about his behavior.

". . . and Jon came out of nowhere!" Frank recapped with their roommates later that night. "I've never seen him that upset."

"Yeah, well, no one messes with my family." Jon stretched out on his bed. "I wish I could say I'm sorry, but I can't. When I saw him hit you . . ."

"Syrus is a big bully in school. I don't know what I would do if he came after me!" Damien said with wide eyes.

Nate nodded. "Yeah, I mean, he's only a grade above us, but he looks like a junior in high school."

"Well, as much as I appreciate what you did, Jon, you can't go off like that. We look too much alike for you to make enemies," Frank said with a slight laugh.

Jon rolled his eyes, but something Frank had said was nagging at him. His brother was right; he had never been that upset before. Why *was* it he'd felt so angry at Syrus? Beyond how much he hated hearing Frank cry for help, seeing him fearful, there was something about it he just didn't know how to process.

He showed up to his next gifts class still confused. McClery was waiting for him at the door, leaning forward on his cane, his face grumpier than ever.

"Oh, so here he is . . . the idiot," McClery said, glaring down at him.

"Excuse me, Liam?"

"Oh no, it's *sir* again until you can learn to act like a civilized young man."

Jon winced. McClery must have been told about his tussle with Syrus. "But—"

"No *but*s! You need to shape up, because there be no sense in me teaching a ruffian. You understand?"

"Yes, sir," said Jon politely.

"All right then, we head to the Sanctuary."

McClery led the way to the bunker, and they traveled down the dark hall to the Oracle Knowledge room, just as they had so many times. Once again Jon found himself staring at the Guardian of Whispers. The statue hadn't changed one bit since the previous lesson.

Recently, his lessons comprised him holding on to the guardian, trying to decipher and separate the images, and discussing them and their implications with McClery. Some prophecies were frightening, while others were quite pleasant. One prophecy was a cure for a terminal disease. Scenes morphed in and out of patients receiving treatment, families crying with happiness, and a doctor in a long white robe shaking hands with a man in a suit in front of a camera. Another prophecy showed a festival with hundreds of people dressed in traditional clothing Jon didn't recognize. They were singing, dancing, holding hands in circles, and feasting with their families.

"Today," McClery said, "as you use the guardian, my boy, your other senses will become more in tune with your gift. You will need to start thinking differently." McClery pulled a tennis ball out of his pocket. "Now, I'm gonna drop this ball, and you will focus on where you imagine it will roll before I drop it. Think hard, Jon."

Jon stared at the yellow tennis ball in the dim light of the dusty bulb above their heads. He focused hard, but nothing came. Eventually, his shoulders dropped. "I don't see anything."

"The inner eye is a tricky thing, Jonny. Go ahead, touch the guardian and focus again."

Jon put a hand on the orb held by the guardian, and once again, he stared at the tennis ball. Shadows started to form around McClery's fingers—a shadow ball falling to the floor and rolling to one side, a ball hitting a wall and bouncing back onto the ground, a ball being stuck back into McClery's pocket.

"What do you see?"

"I see many things, but I'm not sure which one is going to happen." Confused, Jon shook his head and tried again.

"Look for the strongest one. Pick one," the General ordered.

"It'll fall straight down and roll over there." Jon pointed, and a moment later, McCery put the ball in his pocket.

Jon's face dropped. "Wait, that's cheating! You heard which one I said and changed it."

"Oh, really?" McClery said with a smirk. "So, you never saw that possibility?"

"What? Well, no, I did see it," Jon answered, a bit frustrated.

"You don't get to pick the future. As much as you may think you have control, there are too many variables." McClery shook his head and pulled up a chair for Jon. "You know why I was so upset at the fight you got yourself in?"

"No."

"Because, Jonny, you'll find out soon that the gift you

have is even more unique than you thought. You'll have to make very tough decisions." McClery pulled the ball from his pocket and held it up, studying it. "You'll have to pick a future for yourself, and it may not be what you thought it was going to be like. You were foolish yesterday. They say in war, the foolish fight other fools for foolish causes." McClery looked him straight in the eyes. "You can't grow to be foolish, Jonny. Not if you want to survive."

"I don't care about wars or probable futures. Liam, I just want to be great at what I do. I'm not going to be a fool."

"Greatness is inside many people, but some still use it for great and terrible things. That's not the greatness you're searching for, is it?" The older man twirled the tennis ball in his hand and fixed Jon with an intense look.

Jon couldn't take his eyes off the ball as he considered his teacher's words. "No, sir. I want to do great and good things."

McClery lightly tossed the ball in front of Jon's face, then snatched it back, returning it to his pocket. "All right then, boy, we'll see. We'll see."

∩⌒

Despite being behind last term and missing a month of classes, Frank was exceeding his classmates in telepathy studies. He attributed some of his successes to his ability to easily read Jon's mind, which helped him pick up learning techniques at a faster pace.

It felt good to finally start achieving. But ever since break, Frank had noticed Professor Owens watching him more often. What had he done to upset the man? Was he still not performing to Owens's standards? He tried not to let it affect him.

"Sometimes our thoughts are not clear phrases or words," Owens lectured. "Sometimes they are impressions, fleeting and disjointed. I want you to pair up. This time there will be no questions to ask and none to answer. I want you to simply relax with your partner. The first person will just 'daydream,' so to speak. The other will observe and write impressions in their notebook. After this timer goes out"— Owens pulled a large hourglass from a cabinet behind him and set it on the table—"you will discuss what happened and then switch roles. Now find a partner!" He clapped, and everyone moved around the room to pair up.

Frank was the last to find a partner, and the small skinny kid he'd been concerned about during break, Braydon, was the only one left. The boy sat across the table from him as Frank pulled out his notebook and pen.

"All right, you want to go first?" Frank asked.

The boy shrugged. "Doesn't matter to me." He reminded Frank of Peter when he was in his mopey moods.

"I'm Frank, by the way." He put out his hand for a shake, and the boy grasped it limply.

"Braydon," he murmured.

"I guess I'll go first," Frank said.

Owens flipped the timer. Braydon stared at the table as Frank focused on him. Reading minds had become a system for Frank. The first step was to drown out the sounds around him—find the singular voice that would connect him to the mind he wanted to read. It helped that he'd done it with Braydon before by accident. Eventually Frank closed his eyes, blocking out Braydon's appearance and focusing in on the sound of Braydon's mind.

Braydon was remembering something. Frank couldn't get to it at first; the memory was heavy, strong—strong enough that when Frank pushed harder to discover what it was, an image burst through his head. He'd never received images from a person's mind before. He gasped, equally from exhilaration and fear.

Snow blanketed the ground, fat flakes drifting from the sky, but he didn't feel cold. He was looking down, down at a footprint, as if he was looking through Braydon's eyes. A raindrop fell onto his gloved hand, or was it a tear? He couldn't tell. He was holding a photo, and he flipped back the edge to reveal a portrait of a smiling couple. He stroked the faces gently.

"Time's up!" Owens said, loud enough to startle Frank. His eyes flew open, and the images disappeared. Shaken, he quickly scribbled down what he'd seen. Braydon was looking at him expectantly.

"Umm . . ." Frank didn't know what to say. "I got the impression you are . . . sad. Braydon," he said cautiously, and his voice cracked a little, "did you lose someone?"

The boy's eyes got wide and then dropped to the table again. "I don't want to talk about it."

"OK." Frank let it go, and they went on with the lesson as if nothing had happened.

The rest of class was somewhat awkward. Braydon wasn't very talkative and wrote barely anything down after listening to Frank's head. If he had been listening, he would have heard Frank's internal battle about what to do with him. He tried to keep his thoughts from drifting to the subject, but it was a lot harder than one might think.

At the end of class, they turned in their notebooks to Professor Owens, and Frank headed back to Aries house.

They'd been having what the locals called "freezing rain" for three days straight. Frank had never experienced it before; it was like icicles hitting every exposed part of his body. Ice made every walkway slick, but there was no snow, so nothing fun to play in.

When he arrived back at Aries house, huddled inside his

coat, he spotted Jon in the common area. Professor Yang was handing him a list of chores. Part of Jon's detention duty was to clean every inch of Aries house. He'd already spent the last week cleaning the inside and outside of every window. Frank had never seen the windows so clean before. He could actually see out of them!

"Sorry, it's all my fault you have to do this," Frank had said to him a week ago.

Jon had just shaken his head. "No, I'm the reason I'm doing this. But you're worth it, bro!"

Frank took off his coat and put his books away before sitting on the couch with Damien. "What's his duty today?"

"Washing walls, filling holes, and puttying this room. Sounds like he's going to be painting this week," Damien answered, then gave Frank a weird look. "Hey, is everything OK? You feel distressed about something."

"You not supposed to evaluate others' emotions without their permission." Frank teased. They'd all been a little flexible with the rules when it came to their friend group.

"Sorry. You're just sometimes easy to read. Must be because we room together. Professor Vidra says the more time you spend with a person, the more you understand them. So, what's wrong?"

"Do you know Braydon? Fifth grader like us, Taurus house? He's in my telepathy studies class."

"No."

"Well . . ." Frank paused, carefully considering his wording. "He's acting pretty down. I was trying to decide if I should tell a teacher."

"Is he being bullied?"

"No."

"Then don't worry about." Damien put his feet up on the coffee table and stretched out. "Come on, let's sit here and make snide comments at Jon. Hey, Jon! You missed a spot."

Jon glared at them both from atop his ladder.

Soccer tryouts for Aries and Libra house happened to be on the first day it snowed. It wasn't just a dusting either. Jon had woken up with a shiver to discover the ground outside covered in almost six inches. He'd stared in fascination, never having actually seen snow in person. Even though it was cloudy, the snow made it blaringly bright outside. It looked as if someone had draped a clean white sheet over the earth and sprinkled powdered sugar on all the trees.

"You're really going to try out?" Frank asked as they started walking with Mira to the field. Frank and Mira were bundled up in coats, hats, scarves, and gloves. Jon, however, had gone with a lighter jacket and sweatpants. The hem of his sweats collected snow as they traveled.

"Of course! Imagine if I got on the team!" Jon said with a grin. Shivering, he pulled his jacket up over his nose. Once he started running, he would warm up quickly, he was sure of it.

It was almost the end of February, and his detention had finally ended with Professor Yang. Last night he'd dreamed of filling his now empty detention time with practices for the Aries-Libra school soccer team. How hard could it be?

Once they arrived at the field, Jon's confidence waned a bit. Not only were there no fifth-graders, no one younger than eighth grade was at the tryout at all. The teenagers there were at least a foot—and in a couple cases two feet—taller than him.

"There's still time to turn around. I don't think anyone has seen you yet." Frank laughed, and Jon slugged him on the shoulder. "Ouch!"

"Oh, Frank!" Mira shook her head. "Jon, go on. You've come this far. You've got to try."

Jon sucked in a breath and started walking toward the lineup. Whispering giggles from the high schoolers drifted over to him as he got closer. *Confidence—I need confidence!* Jon turned around to see his bundled friends waving at him from the bleachers.

"This, my friends"—he raised a victorious fist in the air—"will be a glorious day!"

"You got this!" Mira yelled back.

It would have been glorious too, if Jon had accounted for the ground freezing after it had been plowed. Instead of showing his great footwork or his speed, he displayed flips onto his butt and his ability to slide into a goal post.

"It's like an ice-skating rink out here. How do you guys do it?" Jon asked a ninth grader who helped him up.

"Welcome to Washington. If you can't play in the rain or cold, might as well never play outdoors at all." The boy laughed. "Maybe in a couple years, kid."

Jon hung his head as they traveled back toward the house.

"It wasn't all that bad," Mira tried to reassure him.

"No. But it wasn't all that good either." Frank smirked.

Mira glared at him. "Jon, why don't you go get cleaned up, and we can go to the Secret Valley?"

This idea did cheer Jon up, and he quickly agreed.

About an hour later, he was bundled up like Frank and Mira and trailing with them through the forest. Jon couldn't help but admire the underbrush, which was dusted with white flakes from the heavy snow-laden branches above.

The hills were hard and slippery, but their group was determined and having too much fun to turn back. They reached the top of the clearing and slid down their makeshift slide, which was faster than usual due to the wet snow. At the bottom they landed with a *thump* and scrambled to the large statue. The cumulation on the statue's hands made the old man appear as if he, too, had been playing in the snow.

"Come on!" Mira dropped to the ground and immediately started swishing her arms and legs apart and together.

"What are you doing?" Jon asked.

"I'm making a snow angel. Join me!" She grabbed the hands of both boys and pulled them to the ground.

Jon did his best to mimic her movements, then tried to get up.

"Stop!" Mira carefully rose to her feet, holding her hands out for balance. Gingerly, she jumped out of the imprint she'd made. "You have to be careful! You don't want to ruin it. Here, give me your hand."

They helped each out of their angels, then looked down at their work. Jon's and Mira's looked like angels, for the most part. Frank hadn't pushed his head down far enough into the snow, so his angel was headless.

Jon smiled. "Oh well . . . it's not that bad."

"But it's not that good either." Mira smirked, and Frank glared at them for a moment before they all burst into laughter.

The Nightmare

CHAPTER 17

"Frank! Help me! Frank, grab my hand!" Jon reached out as he slipped deeper into the mud, a misty fog swarming over him. Through his blurry vision, he could see his brother running away.

Something pulled him from the mud hole with massive strength, but Jon couldn't feel relief—only fear. Whatever it was that had him, it wasn't good. It wasn't there to rescue him.

"No!" he screamed, but it was no use. The intruder snaked an arm around his neck, tightening until Jon gasped for air.

His lungs were starving; he felt dizzy. Spots appeared in his vision. But out of the corner of his eye, on the ground, he thought he saw something. His heart hammered against his ribs as he squinted at it. The hands squeezed harder, and blackness enveloped his vision.

But he could still hear.

"Jon? Jonathan!" a voice called. He could barely hear it, but it sounded worried. "Get Professor Yang!"

Jon felt himself continually drifting toward consciousness, then slipping back under. A face kept blurring in and out of focus.

"Jon? Hey, wake up!" the voice said as Jon's eyes closed again. "Wake up!"

Footsteps running. Crumbling images of faces over him. More footsteps . . .

"Jonathan, honey, it's time to wake up."

"I didn't know what to do, Professor, I've been trying to wake him."

"How long has he been like this?" a frantic voice asked.

"Five to six minutes. I got Levan when I couldn't wake him." The voice that he recognized was Frank's. Why couldn't he wake up? It felt as though a heavy boulder were pinning him down; waking would mean pushing it off, but he couldn't get his arms up. Every muscle in his body was nonresponsive.

"Franklin, help me get him to the medical center. Levan, I want you to wake the nurses. They live in the cottage next to the center."

"Yes ma'am" was all Jon heard before he fell back into the dream.

This time, as the intruder reached around his neck, Jon got his hands up to partially block him, giving himself a little more space to breathe. Waves of panic coursed through his body along with numbing confusion, then stinging betrayal as he remembered Frank running off.

Something sparkled to his left, and Jon peered over as far as he could, cold sweat dripping down his forehead and into his eyes. Blinking, he could just make out a small figure on the ground—conscious or not, he couldn't tell. Then something even more surreal slid into his sight. Before he could really see the item clearly, his eyes popped open, and the vision was gone.

Jon almost jumped from his bed in shock, but a large comforting hand on his chest prevented him. Breathing heavily, he searched the room with his eyes. He was no longer lying on his top bunk. The unfamiliar bed he was in was one of many within the large, strange room, and it was surrounded by people.

Along with the hand on his chest urging him to lie back down, another was pressed to his head. Both belonged to a man he didn't know. The man was whispering to himself with his eyes closed. As Jon relaxed against his pillow, the stranger slowly opened his eyes.

The group gathered around the bed heaved a communal sigh of relief.

Frank laid a hand on his shoulder. "You're awake!"

"Shh . . . lie still, Mr. Reed." The man over him rang out a towel that had been soaking in a bowl on the side table. He pressed the cloth against Jon's forehead. It was hot and felt good, easing Jon's growing headache.

"Wha . . . what happened?" Jon croaked, searching the faces around him for answers. Frank, Levan, and Professor Yang were all there, all in their pajamas.

"You wouldn't wake up." Frank's voice shook. "Professor Yang used her to gift to carry you to the medical center."

"A better question, Mr. Reed, is what happened to you?" The stranger eyed him suspiciously. The man had to be a school nurse. His messy brown hair and thrown-on T-shirt and pajama pants, showing no concern for the below-freezing weather, were evidence of how he must have rushed here after being woken up. "I have never had to calm such a tormented mind in one so young. What is your gift?"

"Umm . . . oracle." Jon's voice sounded scratchy even to his own ears. "What's wrong with my voice?"

"You were yelling for quite some time," Levan said, one of his hands resting on the shoulder of a distraught-looking Frank.

The nurse gave Professor Yang a strange look, and she

nodded.

"OK, boys, Jonathan will be just fine. He'll stay here tonight with Nurse Barrett. Levan, please take Frank back to the house, and tell the other boys to go back to bed."

Frank walked over to Jon and hugged him.

"I'm fine, Frank," Jon reassured him, and he meant it. Honestly, he was feeling a lot better.

Once Levan and Frank left, Nurse Barrett and Professor Yang had a hushed conversation at the foot of Jon's bed. All he heard was the faint whisper, "I already sent him a message. He should be here soon."

Not long after, the doors to the medical center opened, and McClery walked in, leaning on his cane. Unlike Nurse Barrett, he had taken the time to dress in his usual wooly blazer and flat cap. "Min?" Professor Yang met him halfway between Jon's bed and the door, whispering rapidly. "All right, and Mr. Barrett, how is my pupil?"

"My prognosis is that he was dreaming. A nightmare, judging by his yelling." Barrett folded his arms. "I've never experienced anything like this before. I only know what I've read in textbooks, but this . . . this was no ordinary dream."

"No. It isn't possible." McClery paled, and for the first time, Jon saw a glint of fear in his teacher's eyes. "He's too young."

"Too young?" Barrett said sarcastically. "Coming from

you, that is surprising. You should be the first to know that the gift of prophesy is unpredictable."

"There is one way to find out," McClery growled, glancing over at Jon, who propped himself up on his elbows.

"Liam." Professor Yang put a hand on McClery's arm. "You can help him, can't you?"

McClery rubbed her hand, and she smiled. "I'll do what I can, Min. Now, you go back home. You must be freezing. Get those kids into bed, and tell them they'll see their friend in the morning."

She nodded and walked over to Jon, putting a hand on his cheek. "Jonathan, I will check on you in the morning, OK?"

The way she said it—so sweetly, as if she knew everything was going to be OK— made Jon relax a bit. After she left, Barrett pulled a chair up to the bedside for McClery and then retreated to the back of the building.

"So . . ." McClery started, placing his cane in front of him and resting his hands on the golden knob. "Nurse Barrett tells me you had a bad dream."

"I guess I did." Jon put the pillow behind his back so he could sit up and face McClery eye to eye. "It felt strange."

"I would be surprised if it didn't," McClery remarked. "You see, you wouldn't wake up for almost fifteen minutes. Gave everyone a bit of a scare." He tugged a little at his scarf. "Goodness, did Barrett crank up the heat? I'm sweltering in here!" He said the last part loudly, as if hoping Barrett would hear.

"Fifteen minutes? I tried to wake up, but I couldn't. For a while I could hear everyone's voices, but then the dream started again." Jon's hands shook, and McClery glanced down at them.

"Jonny boy, I need you to answer a few questions about this dream." It almost sounded as if he didn't want to ask. "Have you had it before?"

"Yes."

"Is this the one you wrote about?"

"Yes."

"How many times have you had it? Be honest."

"I don't know, maybe five or six times?"

McClery winced and shook his head. "When did they start?"

"I'm not sure. I guess I had one before I came to school."

McClery sighed deeply, the lines in his face deepening. "Why didn't you tell me, boy?" he said quietly. "Did you not trust me?"

Jon didn't want to tell McClery that, yes, he had doubted him at first. "I thought it was just a dream. It *is* just a dream, right? You said it was just a dream."

"Perhaps that is what I hoped it was."

Jon shot McClery a confused look.

"Remember, Jon, when I told you the rarest and strongest way of predicting the future was through dreams?"

"You think I was dreaming the future, Liam?" Jon's voice was barely above a whisper.

"Perhaps. These dreams don't feel normal, Jonny. They feel like the same thing over and over again—sometimes vague, sometimes detailed in things that don't even matter. Some may be related to us, some to others. But they can be very dangerous if you don't know how to interpret them. They feel real, more real than any other dream you've ever had. Is that what it's like?"

"Yes, sir." Jon swallowed. "I'm sorry, I didn't kno—"

"No time for apologizing." McClery's chair creaked as he sat back.

"Sir, why can't I wake up when it happens? It was like I didn't have control over my body or my eyes, like I was fading in and out."

"That, my boy, is because you didn't have control. Your *mind* was in control. Your perceptions were transmitting to you, and you were only the shell for information."

"Has it happened to you before?"

"I have never known foretelling by dreams, Jonny." McClery paused and let that settle in. "But I will help you. I swear it." The man grasped Jon's knee reassuringly—the first genuinely caring physical act he'd ever received from the General. "Now, boy, you must tell me everything about this dream."

In early March, a bulletin announced who had made it to the house soccer team. It was no surprise to Frank that Jon's name wasn't on the list, but Jon wasn't deterred.

"There's always next year, Frank!" he said.

It had been a couple weeks since Jon's nightmare episode—a couple weeks since Frank had been, for the second time, helpless to wake his yelling brother. This latest episode had been even worse than the last, and Jon had needed to stay in the medical center overnight. Professor Yang had been right, though. The next day, Jon was running around the school as his same old self.

It wasn't that easy for Frank to forget. He'd spent many nights over the past week catching up on homework quietly on his bunk, furtively glancing at Jon every few minutes. After the incident, it was Frank who was having trouble sleeping. Of course, he would never tell Jon.

But his brother wasn't the only thing keeping him up at night. Earlier that week after class, Professor Owens had excused everyone for the day except him. Apart from the worry that he was in trouble, Frank had also been frustrated. Staying late after class meant Jon and Mira would have to wait for him, and Jon was sure to be annoyed. They'd planned to meet for a trip to the Secret Valley.

"Mr. Reed, please come up here to the desk," Owens said. When Frank stood in front of Owens's wooden birch desk, he was almost at eye level with his sitting teacher. "I was looking over your notes from the impression exercise a few weeks back. Do you remember it?"

"Not really, sir," Frank said, racking his brain for the journaling log he'd written.

"'I saw snow, like I was Braydon looking down at a photo in my hands.' Are these your words? Does this now sound familiar?"

It all came back to Frank. "Yes, sir. I remember now."

"When I first read this, I was pretty sure you were making it up." Professor Owens's mustache wrinkled as if he had an itch. "But after speaking with young Mr. Burke about the exercise, I believe this encounter actually did happen."

"Sir?" Frank was confused. If Braydon had confirmed the accuracy of his homework, what did Professor Owens want from him?

"What I'm getting at, Mr. Reed, is that this is very advanced work. You not only read his mind but saw a memory—something he hadn't even been thinking about at the time."

"What do you mean, sir?"

"You pulled out a memory of his family. A memory he hadn't even wanted to think about." Owens leaned over his desk, looking into Frank's eyes with glaring accusation. "Who did you learn that from, hmm?"

"What?"

"Was it another professor? An older student? Are you practicing outside of your instruction, young Mr. Reed? Because if you are breaking school rules . . ." Owens pulled his glasses down a bit. He was so close to Frank they were probably unnecessary.

"N-n-no, sir!" Frank said, a bit taken aback. OK, maybe "no" wasn't the whole truth. He had been doing some telepathy with Mira and Jon at the hideout, but nothing like seeing people's memories.

"Hmm . . . you know I can read minds, Mr. Reed?" Owens said, and Frank gulped. "And while you may not have been entirely strict in following the school rules, I can tell you do not know what I am talking about. So be it. You may go . . ."

Frank breathed a sigh of relief; he'd started to sweat a little too. Just as he turned to leave, however, Professor Owens stopped him.

"One more thing, Mr. Reed. If that ever happens again, stop it. Without proper instruction or permission, you could get yourself into a lot of trouble. The mind is a terribly dangerous place to travel in if you don't tread cautiously."

Frank nodded and quickly slipped from the room.

"Sounds like he's scared of your mad skills!" Jon said when he told him and Mira about it later. He was hanging upside down on the statue, his legs wrapped around the gigantic outstretched hands.

"Oh, Jon. Can't you see, Frank? He's just making sure no one's cheating. You did something out of your level. He wants to make sure you aren't breaking school rules." Mira was picking the flowers sprouting around the clearing. March weather had started to warm up the ground enough for a few plants to bloom.

Frank watched his brother swing back and forth. "What about you, Jon? The General helping you with your gift?"

"Maybe? I mean, I haven't had many other dreams—just that one over and over. He says it means something, maybe something about my future, but he doesn't want me to think too heavily on it yet. He's more interested in sitting me in that room with the guardian. It *is* pretty impressive."

"Impressive? Like the Egyptian artifact? The other day, when I was touching it, I saw a man making bricks with clay and water. He was almost naked. Professor Gonzalez said he was most likely a slave from Egyptian times. They would use people to make the bricks for their buildings and not even pay them. Isn't that awful?" Mira angrily plucked several petals from the flower in her hand.

"The guardian is nothing like that. When I'm around the guardian, it's like I'm talking to people like myself. I see things so differently. After using it, I can predict things minutes away without really thinking about it, and there are different choices. The General says we make choices every day that change the future. We just don't notice them because we usually don't know what the future holds."

Frank's mouth dropped open. "Wait, who are you, and what have you done with my brother? You're starting to sound like Nate. Are you really a sage?"

"No." Jon laughed. "I guess I'm just starting to understand why Mom thought it was so important for us to come here. We could change the future, Frank."

"Really?" Frank grabbed Jon's arm and pulled him down from the statue.

Jon landed on his butt with a *thud*. "Hey!"

Frank only laughed. "Didn't see that one coming, did you?"

They all giggled, but Jon's face morphed into an evil grin.

"Oh, no you don't!" Frank ran to the forest line and up the valley slope, Jon hot on his tail.

"Wait for me!" Mira shouted.

All three of them tripped and laughed their way back through the forest and onto the school grounds. Frank almost collided with Damien as he turned the corner to

Aries house.

"Hey!" Frank yelled, almost out of breath. "If Jon asks, don't tell him where I am. He's right behind me." He moved to take off again, but Damien grabbed his arm, his expression serious.

"Frank, wait! Something's happened. I've been looking for you and Jon."

"What's up?"

Jon and Mira appeared behind him, and Frank ducked as his brother tried to put him in a choke hold.

"Stop, all of you!" Damien thrust his hands out to separate them. "Look, they're telling all the students to return to their houses. They don't want any of us leaving until they give the OK."

"Who is *they*?" Jon asked, breathing hard from their run.

"The school administration."

Stolen Relic

CHAPTER 18

After Damien's announcement, Mira ran back to Leo house, and Jon, Frank, and Damien headed into Aries house. All the Aries students were sitting in the common room while Professor Yang checked off names. Levan and the head girl, Sylvia, were giving instructions.

Levan nodded to the boys as they came in. "Just sit down. None of you are to return to your rooms currently. If you need to go to the restroom, you will be escorted by either me or Sylvia. Got it?"

They took a seat next to Nate, who looked at them with a shrug of his shoulders.

"That's everyone," Levan told Professor Yang, and she nodded.

"OK. I'm sure this is just a misunderstanding. I need

to go talk to Professor Mortensen. Levan and Sylvia, keep everyone here." Yang put on a light coat.

"Yes, ma'am," Levan responded.

"What's going on?" an older boy asked.

"Not sure," Levan answered.

"I heard someone broke into the Sanctuary of Knowledge," a girl to Jon's left whispered. Murmurs started to swirl around the room.

"Stop, everyone." Sylvia put her hands up. "We will wait patiently until we hear from Professor Yang. Let's not jump to conclusions."

Almost two hours passed. Several people asked to grab at least homework to fill the dull time, but no one was allowed to leave. Everyone was getting anxious. Just when Jon thought he couldn't wait anymore, Professor Yang, Professor Mortensen, and another man Jon didn't recognize came into the house.

"Levan." Yang rushed over to him. "If anyone has a backpack or any other bag on them, we need to collect them for a search. Please do so gently."

Students who'd overheard were already handing their bags to Sylvia and Levan, who stacked them in an empty room down the hall.

"There has been a theft." Mortensen watched the worried students, the severe expression on his face enough to scare them all into listening. "Your rooms and belongings will be searched, and once they have been shown not to contain what we are looking for, you will be allowed to return to your rooms. As we are going from house to house, you will not be allowed to leave this place until all the houses have been cleared by a school official. Understood?"

They all nodded.

Professor Mortensen and the stranger headed to the back room to start going through each pack, while Professor Yang stayed with the students. The men searched the entire lower portion of Aries house thoroughly, from the closets and study rooms to beneath the tables. Then they moved upstairs.

An hour later they came down from the girls' rooms and headed to the next wing, where the boys slept, but their search there didn't take nearly as long. After about twenty minutes, Professor Mortensen returned to the common room and called Professor Yang over. They talked quietly for a minute, and her face paled.

Jon's stomach dropped in disbelief as she called out names:, "I need to see Nathan, Damien, Franklin, and Jonathan."

∾⌒

The boys were ushered into the gymnasium. More people

followed close behind, including all the teachers, the man who had been with Mortensen, two unfamiliar women, and another man.

"All right, boys," Mortensen said.

Frank had never been so scared in his life. They hadn't done anything wrong, so there was no reason to be afraid, but his legs still shook slightly.

"We will be interviewing each one of you separately. Damien, you go with Professor Owens; Nathan, with Professor McClery; Franklin, with Professor Gonzalez; and I will take Jonathan."

Frank looked over at Jon anxiously, and his brother gave him an encouraging nod.

It wasn't just Professor Gonzalez in the room interviewing; another woman with similar wavy gray hair was there too. She wasn't wearing a school uniform, just black slacks and a button-up blouse.

"Mr. Reed," the other woman said calmly, "I'm Mrs. Altman, from the school board, and you already know Professor Gonzalez. We are going to ask you some questions, and you must answer them honestly." He nodded to show he understood. "Now, do you know why you are here?"

"Umm . . . Professor Mortensen said that someone stole something, and I think they found it in my room, since they called my friends and me here."

"All right, do you know what was taken?" Her eyes burned into his, and Frank easily recognized what she was doing.

"You can read my mind, Mrs. Altman," Frank said, a little sternly. "Why can't you see that I don't know what you're talking about?"

"Franklin . . ." Professor Gonzalez said warningly.

"I'm sorry, Professor, but you've all taught us not to use our gifts on people without asking permission first."

Mrs. Altman put a hand up to stop Professor Gonzalez from replying. "That does not apply to investigations."

"So this isn't an interview. It's an interrogation."

"Mr. Reed, you are right. I can read your mind, and it is blank of the item we're looking for. I can also read that you're confused and upset by this whole thing. What I need you to understand is that a very valuable and dangerous item has gone missing. What was found in your room indicates someone from your house stole it, most likely another boy who sleeps in your dorm. Would one of your friends commit this kind of theft?"

"No, ma'am," Frank said quickly, without a shred of doubt.

"Which one of your friends has been to the Sanctuary of Knowledge?" she asked. "Have they ever talked about it?"

"We've never been to the Sanctuary. Only Jon—" Frank cut himself off.

"Jon?"

"His twin brother," Gonzalez told Mrs. Altman.

"I see. Did your brother talk about anything in particular he was interacting with in the Sanctuary?" Altman pulled out a pen and paper to write notes.

"What are you saying? You think Jon did this?" Frank didn't like where the conversation was going.

Altman calmly opened a file and glanced at its contents. "Answer the question."

"He would never steal," Frank said stubbornly.

"Oh, really? His record here says he's started riots and gets into fights. Is this not a person who would take something that didn't belong to him?"

"No. Never. The only thing he talked about was some stupid statue thing called a guardian," Frank blurted, starting to get upset. He knew she could read his mind for the information anyway.

Altman's eyes grew wide. "Did he talk about this guardian a lot?"

"I don't know. You should ask him. I don't see what this has to do with your investigation."

"It has everything to do with the investigation, Mr. Reed. The Guardian of Whispers—this item your brother has seen and touched—is the artifact that was stolen from the Sanctuary last night."

Now Frank's eyes got wide.

The interview ended soon afterward. Frank didn't want to talk anymore; he was worried he'd implicate his brother. He also didn't know anything about the missing item, so Altman couldn't gain any more information from him. Before he was escorted from the room, Professor Gonzalez patted his hand, giving him a small smile of reassurance.

Nate, Damien, and Professor Yang were waiting for him back at the gym, but Jon was nowhere in sight.

"Come with me, boys." Professor Yang led the way back into the hall. "I'm taking you home."

Frank stopped, planting his feet. "No. Not without Jon."

At that moment, Professor Mortensen's office door opened, and the strong hands of Professor McClery steered Jon out by his shoulders.

Jon! Frank mentally shouted.

Jon turned his head quickly, and their eyes met. *It's OK, Frank. It's a misunderstanding, I'm sure.*

Frank nodded back to his brother as he was ushered out of sight, but the sickening feeling in his gut told him things were far from over.

∩׀⌒

"Where is it?" Mortensen's stern tone was almost threatening. "Jonathan, what you took could be very harmful in the wrong hands."

"I didn't take it, sir," Jon repeated for the hundredth time, but nothing stopped their accusatory questions.

"Oh, really? Then why did we find this in your backpack?" He threw down what looked like a midnight-blue cloth.

Jon ran his finger over it. "What is that?"

"It's the cloth that used to reside underneath the Guardian of Whispers." Mortensen glanced over at the tall, thin man by the door, who walked over and sat in a chair across from him. "Mr. Thurman here is from the school board, and he is a psychic. Mr. Thurman, tell Mr. Reed what you found."

Jon couldn't take his eyes off Mr. Thurman's sickly pale skin or his greasy, slicked-back hair and slightly sunken eyes. The man reminded him of the Grim Reaper.

Mr. Thurman jutted out his pointed chin and pursed his lips. "I saw you, Mr. Reed, using the guardian." Thurman slowly rubbed the midnight-blue cloth between his thumb and forefinger. "Your impression was the freshest, and it was heavily weighted on this cloth."

"That's because I use the guardian with Professor McClery almost every day. I've seen this cloth over a dozen times, but I never paid attention to it. I don't know how it got into my backpack."

"You know what else this cloth told me, Mr. Reed? When I was holding it, I sensed a symbol"—Mr. Thurman had a cruel grin on his narrow face—"the symbol of a ram. The ram of Aries house. That's where we suspected we would find the guardian."

"Well, did you?" Jon challenged, and the men glanced at each other.

"No," Professor Mortensen finally answered. "Jonathan, if you took it, all you need to do is tell us where it is, and we will work out a lighter punishment for the stealing. You have no idea what that thing is capable of."

Jon's hands balled into tight white fists at his sides. "Professor, I didn't take it. Go ahead and read my mind. You'll see I didn't take it."

"People can hide things if they know how, and you know what I see when I read your mind, Jon?" Mortensen leaned down to stare Jon in the eyes. "I see a boy telling his friends how good it felt, how different it made him see the world, when he was close to the guardian. With a motive and evidence like this"—he pointed at the cloth—"we cannot rule out that you broke into my office last night, took the key to the Sanctuary, snuck into the Oracle Knowledge room, and stole the guardian."

Jon's jaw clenched; there was nothing he could say to get himself off the suspect list. Not until he could prove his innocence.

Mr. Thurman slammed the cloth down on the table,

making Jon jump. "If you do not come forward with a confession, then we will have no choice but to call the authorities. There will be harsh punishment and criminal charges, I will make sure of it."

The man leaned over him, his lip curling in disdain. Jon didn't like threats. He also didn't like Mr. Thurman.

Suddenly the office door opened, and McClery came in. "I see, Richard, you wasted no time in cornering my student."

"Liam," Mortensen began, "we have a lot of evidence against Mr. Reed. I would appreciate you stepping out while we—"

"Circumstantial, Richard," McClery interrupted. "I must have a word with you!"

The two men stared at each other for several moments, motionless, until finally Mortensen sighed. "I'll be back, Jonathan. This isn't finished."

McClery and Mortensen stepped out, leaving Jon alone in the office with the Mr. Thurman.

"Funny how things work."

Jon jumped a little. "Excuse me?"

"A boy with such an extraordinary gift." Thurman snaked uncomfortably close to Jon, his voice taking on a devious edge. "A gift probably more powerful than he can control."

Jon stared at his shoes, his skin beginning to crawl. Thurman's hand curled under Jon's chin and pulled his head up, forcing him to look into Mr. Thurman's eyes as the man peered down his nose at him.

"A boy who wastes his time by getting into trouble and taking things that don't belong to him."

"But I—"

"Oh, I know what you're going to say." He ripped his hand away from Jon's chin. "You didn't take it. Well, maybe you didn't. But don't tell me you didn't want too." Thurman leaned down until he was almost nose-to-nose with him, and Jon had to take a step back. "Has McClery told you just how special you are, Mr. Reed?" Jon's eyebrows furrowed in confusion, and Thurman pulled away with a sly smile. "Do you even know who the man is that's teaching you? Oh, how the young trust so easily."

Jon kept quiet. A thousand thoughts flew through his head, none of them making sense. Was McClery untrustworthy? What did Thurman know that he didn't? Mr. Thurman reminded Jon of a snake; why should he listen to him? But he had to admit, when he thought about it, there wasn't a lot Jon knew about McClery. His teacher never talked about himself.

"It's no wonder the guardian is so exciting to you." Thurman sneered, and Jon's palms started to sweat; he felt exposed. "Something just as powerful as you. Strength to combat your own. I hope, Mr. Reed, you weren't the one who took it—for your sake."

At that moment Mortensen and McClery came back into the office, and Thurman slithered back to his chair with a smirk.

"Jonathan," Mortensen said, moving back behind his desk, "I'm afraid I'll have to put you under house arrest until we can find the guardian. Professor McClery will prepare the cottage's extra bedroom as your quarters until we either rule you out as a suspect or you come forward with a confession. You will not be allowed to leave the cottage even for classes until this matter is resolved. McClery will bring you meals and homework." Mortensen turned to leave but then stopped. "I'll call the boy's parents. You can take him, Liam."

Thurman glared at McClery, who shot back a distasteful glance as the school board member stood and crept to the door.

It was silent for a moment.

"Come with me, boy," McClery said gently, putting a hand on Jon's shoulder as they stepped out.

When Jon spotted Frank and received his call, he desperately tried to send a message back to reassure him. An open-mouthed nod from his brother let him know the message had been received.

Not pausing for long, McClery steered him outside the building and all the way to the cottage, along Jon's familiar route. Once there, McClery closed and locked the door behind them, then turned around, his expression unreadable.

"All right, it's just you and me now, boy. This is your chance to explain."

"I didn't do it, Liam," Jon said, offended. "I don't know who did, but it wasn't me."

"OK, OK." McClery raised his hands. "I promised Professor Mortensen I'd be able to get information out of you better than he could." McClery sighed and took off his hat to run a hand through his hair.

"So, that's what this is all about?" Jon waved his hands at the cottage living room. "It's not because you didn't think I did it or because you were protecting me. You just want your precious guardian back!" Jon felt the blood rush to his face, his neck muscles tightening.

"No, boy," McClery said. "I told him that to get you out of that interrogation. To Mortensen, you're already guilty. He can't see anything but the school board looming over his shoulder. Now is your chance. You're going to have to trust me if I'm going to trust you."

"Trust you?" Jon said, his mouth agape. "All right, I'll trust you if you tell me one thing."

McClery stared at him silently, and Jon tried to calm his temper, concentrating on his breathing. "Thurman said I'm more powerful than I know. What did he mean?"

McClery leaned on his cane with a heavy sigh and scratched his chin slowly, studying him. "All right, Jonny, stock the fireplace. You want the details, the truth? I guess you're as ready as you'll ever be."

"Huh?"

"Settle in. We're going to have a little chat."

Shadow Alibis

CHAPTER 19

Aries house was quiet. By the time Frank, Nate, and Damien came back, the common room had cleared out. They hurried up to their own room but were surprised to find it already occupied. Mrs. Altman was sitting in a chair by the window, a notebook and pen in her hand.

Frank eyed her. "What are you doing here?"

"I'm here to check on you," she responded with a twisted fake smile. "Go ahead and get into your bunks, boys."

Cautiously, the boys sat in a row on Nate's bed, exchanging confused glances.

"I just want you all to know you're not in trouble. In fact, you could be a great help if you can think of anything that might lead us to what we're looking for. I know you boys are close, sharing such a small room together."

Frank rolled his eyes.

"I wanted to thank you all for your cooperation during this tough time. Know that the school board is here if you remember anything, even if you think it may get your friend in trouble. It is extremely important to the safety of your friend and this school that we recover this lost item. Just let Professor Yang know you want to talk to me, and she'll make sure it's arranged."

Nothing was said for a full minute. Frank couldn't help the look of disdain he shot toward Mrs. Altman, which she tried to ignore.

"Thank you, Mrs. Altman," Nate said. "We'll let you know if we remember anything."

Mrs. Altman nodded her thanks with a polite smile and left the room. The boys waited silently until they were sure she was out of hearing range, then exploded with stories.

"Oh gosh, I thought I was going to pee myself." Damien pushed off the bunk and started pacing. "Professor Owens spent, like, ten minutes pressing into my thoughts for this guardian thing!"

"They don't really think Jon took it?" Nate asked, watching Damien pace back and forth, his hands on his head. "I mean, we spend almost all our time together, and you're always with him, Frank!"

"I think they want someone to blame, and Jon is an easy

target," Frank said.

"Professor McClery told me that someone stole a key—the key that goes to the Sanctuary," Nate said. "He asked me if I knew where it was normally kept. I didn't know. He had another woman there I've never met. She was just staring at me."

"She was trying to read your mind. I bet she was from the school board. I bet there was a telepath in every interview. I had Mrs. Altman." Frank shivered.

"Well, she can read our minds all she likes. There's no information in there," Nate said, "unless she's interested in zoology. I just finished a book on it."

"I think that's what makes me the angriest." Heat slowly rose up Frank's neck. "None of us have memories or guilty thoughts about the theft, so they're pinning it on the only person who might have a motive."

"Jon." Damien looked around. "Wait, his stuff is missing."

"I don't think they're going to let him talk to anyone until they find what they're looking for," Nate replied.

"Why?"

"It's how they control the situation. If Jon's guilty, talking with his friends could help him hide his actions. We could help him move the guardian or destroy evidence."

"What do you think they'll do to him?" Frank asked, anxious. His brother was his main priority, and right now he didn't even know where he was.

"I'm not sure. I guess check out his alibi, trace his steps. It shouldn't be hard to rule him out as a suspect. He's always with us! We can vouch for him," Nate said reassuringly. "I mean, one of us had to have been with him last night. Right?"

"Not me," said Damien. "Frank?"

Frank shook his head. No, he hadn't been with Jon last night. In fact, he knew Jon had gone off by himself—no one had been with him.

∽⌒

Jon leaned back in the large lounge chair, enjoying the pleasant heat of the fireplace. The shadows dancing on the walls made the living room glow. At the moment, the fire was the cottage's only light source. McClery normally kept it dark; he turned the lights on only if absolutely necessary.

"Comes from owning an old farm. You save money where you can," he'd once said when Jon had turned the lights on during the day to clean.

McClery sat in the large chair across him. After a few minutes of silence, the older man rubbed his eyes. "All right, Jonny, about your question . . ."

Jon waited patiently. He'd learned McClery needed silence to think.

"What Thurman told you has a bit of truth to it." Jon's eyes widened, but his mentor quickly finished with "but not how you think." McClery stared into the fire, his face twisting into a tormented frown. "Have you ever heard the term *Endling*?"

Jon shook his head.

"An Endling is the last of its kind. According to the Perceptually Gifted Society, which is the governing community we operate under, I was an Endling. At least up until they discovered you. Your gift is not only rare, Jonny, it's almost extinct. You received it only though a recessive gene passed down by your great-great-grandmother."

"You mean we're the only oracles alive?" A wash of sadness swept over Jon.

"That we know of, yes. Why do you think everyone looks at you differently, Jonny? Why the school didn't know what to do with you when you arrived? Why they found some lonely old grouch of a farmer from Ireland to come here and teach you, when he can barely understand himself?"

"I . . . I . . ." Was it really true? Did everyone really stare at him? Was his gift strange—strange enough that the school didn't know how to deal with him? "But what about all those prophecies we saw in the Oracle Knowledge room? Who made those?"

"They're all gone," McClery whispered, as if eager to

change the subject. "There were never many living oracles at a time. For some reason we seem to have a shorter lifespan." McClery made a face and stood up. "I'll get us some tea."

Jon watched the flame shadows dance across his socks as his teacher retreated. "So, we're alone."

The whispered words stopped McClery in his tracks.

"They're afraid of us." The older man's voice issued from the darkness behind Jon's chair; it sounded distant, almost sinister. "They don't know how to teach or understand or control our gift, and it worries them. We're unknowns, Jonny. It makes them suspicious."

His footsteps moved away, and Jon sat with the deepening shadows, not only from the fire but from what McClery had shared. The fire crackling and the *clink* of a kettle landing on the stove were the only noises.

Before long, McClery returned and broke Jon's solitude, his chair creaking as he sank back into it. For a few silent moments, Jon studied the man who appeared so unfazed by the truth, the man who'd accepted his fate. As he met his teacher's eyes, Jon realized he'd learned more about McClery in the last half hour than in almost a whole year of classes.

"I believe this fear is why they're so quick to pin this theft on you. You're an easy target, Jonny. You had access, interest, and familiarity with the item that was stolen. You must not hold their accusations against them."

"Why not?" Jon's stomach was roiling with anger. "They don't trust me. Isn't this an attack on me?"

"You're asking the wrong questions. Don't let them get in your head. You're too quick to anger, and we need to think clearly now—think faster and smarter than them. Now, if you want my help, we need to go over the *right* questions, the ones they should have asked first, if they had any sense."

"What are they?"

"First off, where were you last night at twenty hundred hours?"

Jon mentally retraced his steps. Twenty hundred hours . . . that would have been eight o'clock last night. What day was it? Monday. So yesterday was Sunday?

"Sunday nights we go to Mrs. Sniffen's kitchen and help prepare meals for the morning."

"What time did you leave the kitchen?"

"About seven thirty. We usually walk back together, Frank, Mira, and I."

"Good, so you were back at Aries house at eight?"

"No." It came back to him, and he held his breath. Something had been different last night.

As Jon had walked home with Frank and Mira, he'd been overcome by a wave of dizziness. It had been nearing the end of dusk—almost curfew—and a shadow person had appeared in the distance, heading away from campus.

Jon nudged Frank. "Did you see that?"

His brother peered around with a confused expression. "What do you mean? I didn't see anything."

Jon's eyes captured it again a few minutes later, creeping along the side of the school's main building. He couldn't distinguish its features; it was too far away.

"There! I see it again! *Ah!*" Jon gasped as a sharp pain hit his temple.

"I don't see anything," Mira said, searching the same area.

"I saw it, I swear. It was a shadow of someone. They were sneaking."

"Maybe it's a teacher."

"No." Jon's gut was telling him something, and though the shadow person he'd seen may not have actually been there—*yet*—the real person would eventually appear. "I want to check it out."

"No, you can't!" Mira said loudly. "It's almost dusk, and we're supposed to be home."

"Then go home, Mira. Come on, Frank, let's go!" Jon tugged his brother's sleeve, but Frank didn't move. "Frank?"

"Mira's right." Frank shuffled his feet uncomfortably. "You'll get in trouble again, like you always do. You've already been given two strikes. Don't strike out."

"Fine. Go. I don't need you." Jon stubbornly walked away, thinking his brother would follow him, but when he didn't, Jon went on alone.

He waited by the school where he'd seen the shadow, but nothing came. After what felt like forever, he started impatiently walking in circles around the area. Had he imagined it? Usually his visions let him see the shadows within minutes, or even seconds, of when they happened, but this time nothing had seemed to follow the shadow figure.

Just as Jon finally decided to go home, a voice behind him yelled, "Jon! You're out too late!" Levan walked toward him, probably patrolling the area for missing Aries students.

"I'm sorry," Jon said. "I got sidetracked."

"OK. Consider this a warning. Don't do it again."

By the time Jon had reached his room, it had been almost nine. Happy to have avoided getting into trouble, he'd gone to bed early, still wondering what he'd actually seen.

After Jon retold the events to McClery, the man frowned at him.

"This doesn't help your case, Jonny."

"I know. I can see why they think it's me. I've seen the guardian, I've touched it, and now I have no alibi. It would help if I knew what happened."

"Remember when I told you that teachers have to check out the key to the Sanctuary to take a student there?"

"Yes."

"That key is kept locked up in Professor Mortensen's office. There's only one. Last night, Professor Gonzalez had it checked out. The key had been in her school bag, and after class she realized it was missing. At the time, she thought she'd lost it and started retracing her steps. When she arrived at the Sanctuary, she saw the door to the bunker had been left ajar. That was when she ran to get me."

"You're the closest to the bunker."

"That's right. She made her way here, and I went with her to the Sanctuary. We did a room by room search, but the thief had already left. Professor Gonzalez, as a psychic, is an excellent tracker. We traced the thief's steps to the Oracle Knowledge room. When I opened the door, I knew right away what they'd taken." McClery rubbed the back of his neck. "They took nothing else. They only wanted that guardian. It was a planned attack."

"Is that why Mortensen called in the cavalry?"

"*Professor* Mortensen, Mr. Reed," McClery scolded. "Yes. What happened is a criminal action with dire consequences attached to it."

"What do you mean? Professor Mortensen said the guardian was dangerous. What makes it dangerous?" Jon couldn't help feeling worried; he'd used the guardian almost every day.

"The Guardian of Whispers connects with the mind.

Connecting anything to your mind for too long will have side effects, especially for someone trying to use it without instruction. Using it the wrong way can cause strange things to happen—which we can use to our advantage."

"How?" Jon thought about it for a moment. "Oh! We can see if someone is showing signs of using it?"

"Now you're starting to ask the right questions. What other clues do you have?"

Jon thought long and hard. "My shadow," he said, his eyes darkening.

"It's highly unlikely you saw nothing, Jonny, when something sneaky really was going on that night, in the same place you were. What else might we conclude from recent events?"

Jon mentally retraced his steps, asking himself everything the school officials would ask if they thought he was innocent. "How did the cloth get in my backpack?" he asked with a shiver.

"Good question. Where has your backpack been since last night?"

"Home, in my room"—he gasped—"which means it has to be someone in Aries house. A boy, because everyone would notice if a girl was in the boy's wing."

"Good. So, you've narrowed the suspect pool."

"But how are we going to find out who took it? I'm under

house arrest. Wait! You can help me."

"I have to be very careful with what I do and say outside this house, Jonny. Richard almost didn't let me keep you here. Maybe part of him suspects we're in league together. Remember, our kind isn't as trusted as everyone else."

"What about Franklin?" Jon said desperately.

McClery didn't say anything, but a sly smile curling his lips gave Jon his answer: their best hope was his brother.

A Secret Message

CHAPTER 20

A few days had gone by since the incident, and Frank still hadn't seen his brother. Professor Yang had told him and his friends that Jon was still being investigated and was under house arrest with Professor McClery.

"Can we go see him?" Frank had asked, but Yang just gently placed her hand on his shoulder.

"I'm sorry, but they're allowing him to see only school staff until this is settled." She paused. "And I hate to tell you this, boys, but they've also told me that the three of you are to attend your classes and meals only. The rest of your free time will be spent in Aries house."

"What?" they all exclaimed at once.

"I thought they believed we didn't have anything to do with it?" Damien said.

Professor Yang raised her hands. "Unfortunately, it's not up to me, boys."

"They think we have too much loyalty to Jon." Nate had glared at her, and she'd stared down at her feet.

"I'm positive someone will come forward soon."

So, for several days, the boys had gone to class, then the house, then to dinner, then back to the house. Everyone was whispering about them—mostly about Frank. Other students couldn't tell him and his brother apart. Hushed voices and pointed fingers surrounded them every day, wherever they went, and no one sat at their table anymore except Mira.

"My father didn't want me to talk with you," Mira told them at lunch one day, "but I don't care. I told him what I thought about Jon taking the guardian. I told him it was ridiculous!"

It was no longer a secret what item had been taken. Mortensen had made many announcements during meals asking people to come forward with information, but it appeared everyone was just as clueless as Frank had been during his interrogation. Even the teachers were flustered and anxious. Professor Owens wouldn't look at Frank, and when he had no choice but to talk to him, he stumbled over his words.

Every night before collapsing into bed, Frank prayed they

would clear Jon's name soon. Being away from his brother and being watched at every turn were wearing on him.

On Friday, Frank was called to Mortensen's office to take a call from his parents.

"Is Jon OK?" Mom asked, her voice heavy with concern.

Frank could feel Mortensen's eyes on his back as the superintendent listened in on the conversation. "They won't let me see him until after this is over."

"Professor Mortensen says they have evidence Jon took this artifact," said Dad.

"If they did, Jon wouldn't still be under investigation. Jon didn't take it," Frank told him. "He may get into trouble a lot, but not like this. He's not a thief."

"I'm coming up there to settle this," Dad said.

"Harvey, I don't think there's much we can do right now," Mom interjected. "The school board has every right to suspend Jon's activities if they think he's done something at a criminal level. We're lucky he's just under house arrest for now. It means they're still looking for answers."

"How bad is it, Frank—the case against Jon?" Dad asked.

Frank glanced over at Mortensen. He didn't want to lie to his parents, but he also didn't want them to worry, and he definitely didn't want to help the man watching him build a better case against his brother.

"The case is full of holes." Frank's gaze never left

Mortensen, who didn't blink. "I'm sure they'll catch who did this any day now. The school is working hard to find the truth."

"All right, Frank. We get to talk to Jon soon. I just want to make sure you're OK." Mom's kind, smooth voice gave Frank strength—strength he normally borrowed from Jon, if he was there.

"I'm good, Mom. Still doing my homework and behaving myself. I love you guys."

Even though the phone call was brief, it was nice to hear his parents' voices. He hadn't seen them since Christmas, almost three months ago, and the letters he received couldn't replace his mother's hugs or playing catch with his dad.

Right now, school wasn't a fun place to be, and he dreamed of home every night.

On Saturday, the boys traveled to lunch together, Levan walking beside them to make sure they made it to the hall and back. At least during meals they were allowed some unchaperoned time, when Mira joined them, but the routine was already getting old.

Kevin, their friend from PE, walked by their table and leaned down to pick something up. "You dropped this." He extended whatever it was to Frank.

"I didn't drop anything," Frank said. Then his gaze fell to the small action figure in the boy's hand. "Oh, yes, that!

Now I remember. Thank you." He took it in his hands, and Kevin walked off.

Damien leaned in to see. "What is that?"

"It's a message," Frank said, and he put the toy down on the table.

It was an action figure of Han Solo.

∩∣⌒

Jon had spent many days locked up in the cottage. His teachers came by to drop off assignments, administer tests, and lecture occasionally, if needed. But even with all the comings and goings, he'd never felt so alone.

Every meal, McClery brought his food from the cafeteria and ate at the dining table with him. In the evenings, Jon would beg his teacher for any news about the theft, about his friends, and especially about Frank.

"They're watching your friends." The old man rubbed his eyes with a weathered hand. "They're only allowed to go to class and meals. The rest of their time is spent at Aries house. No new leads on the case, except for the fact they've searched almost every nook and cranny of the school. I think their next step is to start pulling apart the grounds."

"Liam, I've been thinking. I need to get a message to Frank." Jon had been considering how to get a message to his brother for days. "I need to tell him what to look for. I need to get the information about the guardian's side effects to him somehow."

"I can't walk up to Frank, Jonny. Not right now. He'd be pulled in for questioning."

"I know that." Jon dug around in his backpack. "But I've seen you with Professor Yang, your friend, and I bet she would help!"

"All right, say I give your message to Professor Yang. What if someone stumbles on it, and it gets her and I both in trouble? Your message must be cryptic."

Jon nodded and pulled a toy out of his bag. "I have a plan! I just need your help. You're more familiar with gifted people than I am," He put the action figure on the table. "Mira is a psychic. I need to place a strong impression into this that she can read. You've got to help me."

McClery looked skeptical at first but then grinned slyly. "All right, boy, how good is this psychic friend of yours?"

"I think she's the best."

∩∣∩

"What does it say? I don't see a message." Damien grabbed the action figure and turned it around in his hands. "Is it written on it somewhere?"

"No!" Frank pulled it away from him again. "I need to think . . ." The action figure was Jon's favorite toy—Han

Solo, his hero. Maybe Jon was saying Frank needed to be the hero now, that it was his turn to take the lead. "I'm not sure what it means, but I think Jon needs our help."

"Here, Frank, let me look." He handed it over to Mira, but no sooner had she wrapped her hand around it than she dropped it with a gasp. "Oh . . ."

"What?" Damien asked.

"She sensed something." Nate's eyes widened, and he smiled.

"You were right, Frank. Jon definitely sent this to us for a reason," Mira said quietly, her eyes glued on the action figure.

"Please, Mira, you have to help us. You have to find out what he wants," Frank begged, and Mira nodded.

"I'll take it home." She wrapped the toy in her napkin and put it in her backpack. "The Leo-Aquarius team has a soccer match this afternoon against our rivals, Scorpio-Taurus. Everyone will be at the game, and I'll have privacy. It'll take time."

"Good, then we'll meet again at dinner tonight," Frank said, excited. Finally they were doing more than just sitting on their hands. "We have to keep this to ourselves."

They all agreed, and once lunch was over, Levan walked them back to the house.

Several soccer matches had been going on that day, but

they'd missed every single one. The Aries-Libra team were going up against the Capricorn-Virgo team in their second match of the year. It was supposed to be a great game, and all the students from Aries house had gone to watch, which left the boys with the house almost to themselves. They sat in their room to discuss the message, keeping their voices low.

"What do you think it'll say?" Damien asked. "Maybe it'll have the name of who took the guardian."

"I think if Jon knew who took the guardian, he wouldn't still be under house arrest," Nate said, rolling his eyes.

"Maybe it's directions to where he hid the guardian?"

"Damien!" both Nate and Frank said, shocked.

"What?" He looked at them knowingly. "It *is* a possibility—"

"Oh boy . . ." Frank sighed.

Later that night at dinner, Mira sat down with Frank and the others.

"All right, where is it?" Frank asked. "Spill."

"I'm sorry, Frank, but I buried it. I didn't want anyone finding it. The impression was strong enough that it could get us all in trouble."

"What did it say?" Nate asked.

"It was weird." Mira looked at them, pulling out a small piece of paper. "It was just words. They were repeated over and over again. Five different words: *boy*, *Aries*, *dizziness*, *hallucinations*, and *paranoia*."

"Sounds like he's trying to describe someone," Nate commented, "perhaps a suspect."

"Sounds like someone who's lost their marbles," Damien added.

Frank slapped him on the back. "You're right, Damien!"

"I am?"

"Well, not in the way you were talking about. Dizziness, hallucinations, and paranoia all sound like symptoms."

Damien sat up straighter and smirked, obviously proud of himself.

"So, we're looking for a sick person?" Mira asked, confused. "I don't know of any. Do you guys?"

"Maybe it's not that they're sick in the traditional sense but that they'll start acting that way," Nate mused, and Frank could almost watch the boy's wheels turn.

Damien cocked his head. "Huh?"

"You know how they told us the guardian was dangerous?"

A light bulb went off in Frank's head. "These must be symptoms of being exposed to the guardian. We should be able to look for these signs."

They all got quiet and went back to eating their food as Professor Owens passed by, stopping purposefully to peer at them. They waited until he was out of hearing range before

GUARDIAN OF WHISPERS

continuing.

"How are we going to look for this boy? We're being watched like hawks!" Mira said angrily.

"You're right." Frank's head spun with thoughts. What would Jon do? No, he needed to stop thinking about what Jon would do and start thinking about what *Frank* would do. "It's an Aries boy, right? We'll just keep our eyes open in the house. Mira, you have more freedom than us. You'll watch for signs outside Aries house. And don't forget, we all have classes too."

"But you guys are the only Aries boys in my classes. I already keep an eye on you." She smirked, making them all blush.

∩⏜

Jon thought a lot about his Han Solo message in the days that followed. Over the weekend, he'd been visited by Professor Mortensen, who had informed him and Professor McClery that Jon was to appear before the school board Monday night. Mortensen's stay had been short and blunt, leaving Jon with his nerves on edge.

"What do you think will happen?" Jon asked McClery once Mortensen left.

"I think they've completed their search and have come up empty-handed. Min told me the school board is four against one in believing you're the culprit. They'll want to appeal to you, maybe give you a deal to come forward, then end with a threat." McClery set a plate of food in front of Jon at the dining table.

"What type of threat?" Jon asked. He'd suddenly lost his appetite.

"Expulsion, maybe harsher punishment. They don't have enough to convict you of any crime yet, but they're worried about the guardian ending up in the wrong hands. They may have to involve the society if it's not found."

"How so? Liam, what is everyone so afraid of?"

McClery just pointed at his food. "Eat, boy. It's a story for another time."

Monday night came quickly. McClery escorted Jon to the school and then into the assembly room. A long table had been set up at the end, and seated at it was the school board.

McClery put a hand on his shoulder. "Jonny, you know Mr. Thurman, Professor Mortensen. That there is Mr. Camacho, Ms. Fernandes, Mrs. Altman, and Ms. Graham."

Jon's eyes darted between group. Someone didn't think he was responsible for the crime, but he couldn't tell who. They all stared at him with very serious faces. Mr. Camacho looked a lot like his daughter—hazel skin, short wavy brown hair. Mr. Thurman, Jon knew, believed him guilty; he'd learned that early. Mrs. Altman wore her hair in a tight bun and had on a gray blazer. Ms. Graham and Ms. Fernandes were both gray-haired, and their flowery-patterned blouses reminded Jon of something his aunt Gladys would wear.

"Have a seat, Mr. Reed." Mortensen pointed to a solitary chair.

Jon made his way over to it. The *creak* as he sat down echoed through the nearly silent room.

"Now, Mr. Reed, we have confirmed that you were alone the day of the theft, that the cloth the guardian sits on was found in your backpack during our search. Mr. Thurman sensed your impressions on the cloth in question. You have expressed to your friends your fascination with the Guardian of Whispers, and you knew where it was kept in the Sanctuary of Knowledge and how teachers checked out the key. Tell us, how do you address these circumstances surrounding the missing guardian?"

Silence settled over the room. Jon glanced over at McClery, who smiled at him. With his chin lifted, Jon looked each school board member in the eyes as they waited on his answer.

"Sir, I would also like to know how the cloth got into my backpack. If I'd taken the guardian, I would never have left something like that in a place where it would be found so easily. I also would never have taken the cloth in the first place. That's just another thing to hide, don't you think? I wouldn't be very smart if I did those things, would I?"

Most of the board members looked slightly shocked, but Thurman just glared at him.

"Are you mocking and disrespecting this board, Mr. Reed?" he asked.

"No, sir. I mean no disrespect," Jon said. "I'm just asking the right questions. I know I didn't take the guardian, so I'm confused about how the cloth got into my backpack when it was at home the entire time. I would also ask *why*? Why would someone take the guardian?" Thurman huffed at that. "I admit, I am fascinated by the statue, but I had access to the guardian almost every day. Why would I need to take it home with me?"

"Maybe you didn't take it, Mr. Reed," Mrs. Altman said, considering him, "but you can't deny you were gone that night, and no one can corroborate your story."

"That is true, ma'am," he said carefully, "but I didn't take it. There must have been someone else out past dusk that night. There would be record of that student not being in their home. I hope the board is looking at them as well."

Mr. Thurman's face was getting red. "Are you insinuating that we haven't been looking at this case from all angles?"

"No, sir. Again, I'm sure the board is doing everything they can to make sure the truth is revealed." Jon straightened a little in his chair. "I just ask that they also consider evidence that may not support their suspicions." A few members of the board tilted their chins in understanding. "Please, if I may, I'd like to ask those members of the board who are able to read my mind to see if I'm lying or hiding anything."

There was silence for several minutes as the school board stared at him. Even Mortensen was quiet and pensive. Mr. Camacho was smirking at Jon.

"Enough of this!" Thurman burst out in a huff. "Richard?"

Mortensen took a breath. "Mr. Reed, we are going to be considering your case in particular on Thursday. If there are no new developments or if the guardian is yet to be found, the school board will have to vote on whether or not to revoke your admission. You are excused."

The culprit
CHAPTER 21

A visitor came to Aries house on Tuesday while Damien, Nate, and Frank were sitting in the common room scouting out their fellow Aries for any suspicious signs. Professor Yang spoke with the man at the door, then pointed in their direction. Nodding, the stranger walked toward them and settled comfortably into the chair facing the couch they were sharing.

"Mr. Franklin Reed?" he asked, and Frank stared at the oddly familiar face. "I am Mr. Camacho." The boys shared glances. "Mira's father."

"I know who you are," Frank said quietly.

"Then you know I'm a school board member looking for the missing artifact."

"Jon didn't take it," Frank said sternly. He didn't care if

the man was Mira's father; he was also a person wrongfully accusing his brother.

"I'm beginning to believe that too." Mr. Camacho laughed as the boys' eyebrows shot up. "What I'm saying is, I'm not sure it was Jonathan. But the board isn't leaning his way, and we're deciding on Thursday if he gets expelled. I just thought you should know."

Frank couldn't believe Mr. Camacho was passing them information. Could it be there were doubting members on the school board?

Mr. Camacho didn't stay to answer their questions. He nodded politely, to them as he left.

"We need to speed up our search!"

That night they ramped up their efforts. Damien sat in the common room and outside all the boy's rooms trying to sense feelings of students within. At one time, Damian thought he felt a strong sense of confusion and doubt from one room, but Levan had popped up and Damien quickly made an excuse to sneak away.

Nate was scribbling notes about everyone in the house, he had a journal full of his observations.

"I made sure to write it in a complex code in case it fell into the wrong hands." Nate told him.

And while Frank knew he wasn't supposed to, he continued using his gift in the house to read the mind of everyone he met. Ironically, the continuous practice was paying off in class; he was breezing through school assignments.

On Wednesday, when Professor Owens was lecturing, Frank casually let his mind wander into the thoughts and impressions of his classmates. A girl in front was dreaming about flowers. Some students were thinking about what Owens was saying. Another girl was thinking about last weekend's soccer match.

Then a weird impression drifted through his head, almost like an image. It was of a hand stroking something metal. The hand was shaking; the thoughts were a series of nervous *should*s and *should not*s. Frank sat up straighter, looking around the room. *What was that?*

He refocused on his classmates' minds until he found the metal object again. *Look closer*, he begged the mind he was reading.

Suddenly, the object came into focus.

The Guardian of Whispers! At least, that's what it looked like based on Jon's description. Someone in his class had it! A telepath!

Frank surreptitiously scanned his classmates. In the corner, a kid was rocking slightly back and forth, rubbing his head and obscuring Frank's view of his face.

"Mr. Reed are you paying attention?" Professor Owens

said sharply.

"Sorry, Professor," Frank mumbled. He turned his gaze back to his notes, his heart racing. When he closed his eyes and tried to lock on to the mind again, he'd lost focus.

After class, as the students stuffed their notebooks and homework pages back into their backpacks, Frank quickly searched for the student he'd seen earlier, but the spot where he'd been sitting was now vacant. Disappointed, Frank turned quickly to leave but bumped into another student, Braydon, who dropped his book bag as they collided.

"Oh, I'm sorry." Frank reached down to pick up the boy's bag, but Braydon swiped it up before he could.

"It's all right, I got it," Braydon said.

The image again—the metal object appeared in Frank's mind. Was the kid still in the room?

"Can I ask you a question?" Frank said.

Braydon paused, throwing his bag on his shoulder. "It has to be quick. I have to meet someone at Gemini house." He shoved his hands in his pockets.

"Where did you sit in class today?"

"That's a weird question. Somewhere over there." Braydon gestured vaguely in a general location.

"Wonderful! Did you see anything strange? Like a student who wasn't acting normal?"

Braydon shook his head, rubbing his temples as if he had

a headache. "Sorry, no. I really need to go. Bye, Frank." He rushed off with a wave.

Frank took a step forward, and something crunched under his foot. He looked down to see a rather nice pen on the floor. Maybe it was Braydon's?

"Braydon, wait!" Frank picked the pen up and ran to catch his classmate, but he was already gone. If Frank saw him later, he would try and return it, but in the meantime, he mindlessly put it in his pocket. He had to talk to the others.

That evening at dinner, Frank told them all about his episode in class.

"So, they're a telepath. Someone in your class?" Damien repeated excitedly, bouncing a little in his chair. It was their first real break.

"I wish you'd gotten a better look at the kid in the back," Mira commented, frowning slightly, "but it doesn't make a lot of sense. You're the only Aries boy in your class."

"Yeah, didn't Jon tell us it was an Aries boy?" Damien said. "You must have read their mind wrong. Maybe they were thinking about something else, like a metal baseball bat."

"No. This was different. I read them fantasizing about it—like they missed touching it and had to get back to it. I've never seen the guardian before, but it looked just like Jon described it." But Mira was right; he *was* the only Aries boy in his class. Had they been searching the wrong house the entire time? It would explain why they had yet to come up with potential suspects.

"But Jon said—" Damien started, but Frank stopped him.

"Jon has been known to be wrong," he said sternly, and his friend closed his mouth. "I feel very confident in what I saw."

"Frank, do you realize what you're saying? You read someone's memory?" Nate's jaw dropped. "That's really advanced for someone our age. Have you read a memory before?"

"Yeah, actually." Frank pulled out his notebook and flipped to his pages from just after Christmas break. "I read my partner's memory during an assignment."

"Who was your partner?" Mira asked.

"Braydon. I read a strong impression related to his parents, I think, but I'm not sure." Frank sat up straight as a thought occurred to him. He pulled the fancy pen from his pocket. "I ran into Braydon right before I sensed the guardian memory a second time. Mira, he dropped this when he rushed out. Does it tell you anything?"

He put the pen in her hand, and she closed her eyes, wrapping her fingers around it.

"I feel cold," she whispered. "I sense snow."

"It's Braydon," Frank murmured, but Mira opened her

eyes to glare at him. "Sorry."

Closing her eyes again to regain her focus, she pressed the item tightly between her hands, rolling it back and forth slowly. All the boys kept an eye out for anyone watching. They would all get in trouble if they were caught.

Suddenly, Mira dropped the item as if it had burned her. She looked around at them all, her hands covering her mouth in surprise.

"It's him, Frank," she whispered with wide eyes. "Braydon took the guardian."

∩∩

Jon sat at the dining table while McClery placed another sticky note on the wall. This one had a single word scribbled on it. *Why?*

A dozen or more questions already filled the wall, along with a makeshift timeline.

"It's no use, Liam. There's no way we're going to figure this out by tomorrow. I might as well start packing my bags." Jon rubbed his eyes; his brain was fried from staying up the last two nights. "I hoped Frank would have found something by now. We've just run out of time."

"Who are you?" McClery asked him.

"Excuse me?"

"I asked you a question, boy. Who are you? Because you sure aren't Jonathan Reed. You sound like a quitter, and that isn't the Jonny I know." McClery smirked, then pulled the Post-it back off the wall and smacked it down on the table in front of Jon. "Why?"

"Why . . ."

"Why, Jonny, would someone take the guardian? What would they need it for?" McClery asked, as if the question had just occurred to him. "Why would anyone take it?" He mumbled but Jon lifted his head to listen.

"Maybe they are an oracle too, a hidden one?" Jon offered, and his mentor shook his head.

"Perhaps, but unlikely."

"Someone interested in oracle history? Maybe a future they want to find out about?"

"There is no easy way to pull those images, well unless you're specially trained. No student would be able to do it—except you, of course, but you have the gift. I guess at some level, certain gifts could pull images from it, but it would be very risky. We don't know what the results would be. They could end up destroying themselves and much more."

Jon leaned back in his chair, exhausted. "I wish we knew why. I think that would solve a lot of questions."

∩∣⌒

"This is good. All we have to do is tell a teacher!" Damien said on their walk to Aries house. Levan was a good distance behind them; he seemed to be getting tired of his daily duties.

"We can't do that!" Nate exclaimed, barely keeping his voice down. "How do you suppose we tell them? We need more evidence, or they're going to think we planted the guardian on Braydon. We have to catch him in the act!"

"All right, Mr. Smarty Pants." Damien crossed his arms. "How do you think we catch Braydon without being able to move about the school?"

"We do it at night," Mira said. All the boys looked at her as if she were crazy. "No, think about it. How else is Braydon managing to use the guardian? He must do it at night when no one is up to see him. I bet he sneaks out after roll call. Our best chance of finding the guardian and catching Braydon is to do it at night."

"Then it has to be tonight," Frank said, to the whole group's shock. "It *has* to be. Tomorrow they'll expel Jon or worse."

Silence settled over the group as they gradually slowed to a stop.

"If you guys won't help me, it doesn't matter," Frank said quietly. "I'll do it by myself if I need to."

No one said anything for another moment, then Mira reached out and took his hand. "Tonight," she said, smiling confidently at him.

Nate put his hand over theirs. "Tonight."

They all looked over at Damien, who still had his arms crossed.

"All right, tonight." Damien reluctantly added his hand to the stack. "If we all end up in detention for the rest of our school years, I'm blaming Jonathan Reed."

The Plan

CHAPTER 22

The plan was far from foolproof. There was no guarantee Braydon would even be going out that night, although, based on the impression he'd read from his mind earlier, Frank was fairly confident he would be. It seemed as though Braydon had been having urges in class, like an addict. They would find him, he was sure. They had to.

Frank, Damien, and Nate all waited in their room until lights out and then quickly headed to the window. It was a story down, with only bushes below to catch them. Mira was waiting on the ground with a large ladder.

"Where did you get that?" Damien whispered down, and she put her finger to her lips.

"No questions, just get down here." She waved.

Damien climbed out first, with Mira holding the bottom

of the ladder. Once they were all on the ground, they hid the ladder up against the house behind some bushes and started taking the back trails to Gemini house.

"I got permission to help with kitchen duty tonight. I asked Mrs. Sniffens if I could finish washing the counters and then lock up. She let me borrow her key." Mira held it up. "I got the ladder from the custodian closet. We'll have to put it back tonight before anyone notices."

Damien narrowed his eyes at her. "How come they haven't noticed you aren't back from helping Mrs. Sniffens?"

"Oh, that's because Professor Vidra, my house master, got a note from my father saying I was very ill and spending the evening in the medical center." She smiled, and Nate shook his head.

"We are going to be in so much trouble." Damien started biting his nails.

"Not if we find the guardian," Frank said, and pointed to Gemini house ahead. They all paused when they noticed the door was slightly ajar, a piece of tape holding the latch back from locking. "He's already left," Frank whispered.

They scurried around the back of the house to think.

"Now what?" Mira asked. "Which direction would he have gone?"

"I'm not sure."

Nate adjusted his glasses. "There is one way to find him."

"Oh, really? How, Smarty?" Damien asked.

"You dummy"—Nate rolled his eyes—"you're an empath, right?"

"What?"

"He's right, Damien. Can't you sense where he's gone?" Mira asked.

Damien shook his hands in front of him. "Look, I'm barely an empath. I can only sense, like, really, *really* strong emotions."

"Well, I don't think Braydon's emotions could be any stronger than they are now," Frank said encouragingly. "Look, you've always wanted to use your gift for something cool. Now's your chance!"

"OK . . ." Damien frowned, stretching his neck and arms as if preparing for a race. "I guess I can at least give it a try." He closed his eyes and wrapped his arms around his body.

"OK, Damien, you'll be looking for feelings of paranoia, fear, guilt, maybe even excitement," Nate said quietly.

"And need," Frank added. "I got the impression he *needed* to be with the guardian, like he was addicted to it."

Damien nodded but didn't open his eyes. He took a few deep breaths. For several minutes, nothing seemed to be happening, but after a while, Damien's eyebrows furrowed, and his neck craned slightly to the left.

"This way?" he said, sounding undecided.

That was good enough for Frank. They slowly made their way toward a trail into the forest.

The woods were dark, and no one had brought a flashlight, but the moon was large and the sky clear, so the light cascaded onto the forest floor in uneven patches. Mira held Frank's hand, while Frank kept track of Damien by keeping one hand on his friend's shoulder. Nate took up the rear, and they traveled quietly and cautiously so they didn't trip.

After a short distance, Damien abruptly stopped and put his hands on his hips, looking around.

"What is it?" Frank whispered.

"I lost it. I'm sorry. I probably took us in the wrong direction in the first place . . ." Damien said sadly, but Mira pulled on Frank's shirt.

"No, look!" she hissed. Ahead, a light flickered through the trees. They all shared a shuddering breath. "We've found him."

They decided to split up and come at him from different angles, in case Braydon chose to run. As he approached, Frank could just make out the tiny figure of a boy at the base of a large tree. A flashlight off to the side was pointing toward the sky, and the boy's hands were resting on an object. Braydon appeared to be moving slightly, but it was hard to tell in the dark.

"Braydon?" Frank said quietly as he got closer.

No response. Braydon continued rocking slightly back and forth, oblivious to Frank's presence.

"Braydon?" Frank was right in front of him now. He crouched down to look into his classmate's eyes, but they were glazed over. "Braydon!"

His concerned voice brought the rest of his friends forward quickly.

"What's wrong?" Mira asked, out of breath, and Frank shook his head.

"I don't know. He isn't responding to me."

"Maybe we should take the guardian out of his hands?" Nate suggested.

Frank and Nate both grabbed the object, and it slipped out of Braydon's fingers. But during the two seconds his hands were touching the statue, a rush of images overwhelmed Frank's mind, and he dropped it. Nate followed suit.

"What was that?" Frank felt as if his heart were pounding a thousand beats per minute. Nate was also breathing hard, his glasses askew.

"I don't think it's meant for us," Nate said, staring at the guardian.

"What happened?" a voice asked.

Frank shook his head and sat up to look at Braydon, who was running his hand through his hair in confusion.

"What happened?" Damien repeated. "You stole the Guardian of Whispers! You've been hiding it here and using it. I think the better question is, what were you thinking?"

Braydon stared at them, continuing to rub his face and hands. "I can't . . . I can't think . . ." He let out a yell and collapsed by the tree, shaking.

"Help!" Mira shouted, gripping Braydon's shoulders as he seized.

"No," Nate said, "don't hold him down. Just move things away from him." They grabbed the flashlight and stood back.

"What are we going to do?" Damien said. "I'll get help!"

As Damien took the discarded flashlight and headed back through the forest, the rest of them stayed to watch over Braydon. Eventually he stopped shaking and went limp.

Nate frowned, putting a hand on Braydon's head. "I don't know if Damien's going to make it back in time."

"What's happening to him?" Mira asked, her voice quivering.

"I don't know. I think it has to do with using the guardian. It isn't meant for us. We're not oracles. I bet using it with other gifts has horrible side effects." Nate pulled back one of Braydon's eyelids and examined the whites of his eyes. "Mira, help me rub his arms. Maybe we can wake him!"

Frank raked his fingers through his hair; he had to think of something, *anything* that could be useful. His memory flashed back to the last time he'd needed help. Mira had been confronted by that bully, Syrus. Frank had interrupted only to land in the middle of a fight. His mind had called out for help, and a few seconds later Jon had appeared. Was it possible he'd sent a message? Was it possible his silent plea had been heard by the one person he was closest too?

It might work, it might not, but Frank had to try something.

"Should we put something under his head?" Mira was asking Nate, but Frank's focus was elsewhere. He let the scene fade into the background and concentrated on sending one word—just one word—to his brother, to anyone.

Help. Please help!

He focused every ounce of his energy on sending the message. They were far into the woods, far from the school, far from his brother.

Help, Jon. Please help.

The Mystery

CHAPTER 23

Jon woke with a start. Something was wrong.

He tore off his blanket, headed into the hall, and knocked on the door opposite his. "Liam! Liam!" Jon's head swam, and he almost collapsed into McClery's arms when his teacher opened the door.

"What is it, boy?" McClery flipped on the lights and lowered Jon to the floor.

An image was racing through his head—Frank and another boy he didn't recognize. Frank was yelling, crying. *Help. Please help!*

"Liam, Frank needs us!" Jon's voice quavered at he tried to stay conscious. The flurry of images in his mind wasn't letting up. "Please help. He needs help."

"Where are they?" McClery asked without hesitation, his

hands resting on Jon's shoulders.

Jon's arms were shaking now. "I don't know."

"Ask him!"

"I don't know how," Jon whimpered.

"Yes, you do, Jonny." McClery shook his shoulders. "Just think it. Frank will answer."

McClery dashed out, and Jon thought the question over and over, just as he had during his brother's practice sessions. *Where are you?*

The forest. Jon, hurry. *Bring help.*

McClery came back with shoes and a coat. Quickly, he threw a pair of shoes to Jon, who pulled them on and stood, his legs wobbling.

"The forest! I think someone is hurt," Jon said

McClery gave him a nod, and they tore from the house at a run. Limping, McClery headed straight for the medical center. He knocked on the door of a small cottage next to it, and Nurse Barrett answered.

"Liam, what in all things—" He spotted Jon in his pajamas. "Had another episode?"

"No. There's a boy hurt in the woods." McClery turned and headed to the forest trail Jon pointed to, and Barrett pulled on a coat and boots. As they reached the forest's edge, another boy came hurtling toward them.

"Damien!" Jon cried.

The boy stopped in surprise. His face was scratched and dirty, as if he'd fallen a couple of times during his run through the forest to get to them. "Help us! It's Braydon. He's sick!"

No one asked what they were doing out so late. No one asked why they were in the woods, no one even asked what happened. Nurse Barrett only asked where and they were off.

Jon hadn't prepared to trek through the woods, but the rubber boots McClery had handed him weren't doing a bad job. He tried hard to follow McClery's lead, as he was the only one with a flashlight, but roots everywhere in the underbrush tripped him up, and keeping himself from falling was a constant effort. But despite the darkness and difficult terrain, they found the group of huddled kids without much trouble.

Barrett rushed in front, kneeling by the unconscious boy's side. "What happened?" he asked, putting his hands on the boy's chest.

"He was using the guardian, sir." Nate pointed to where it lay on the ground, the orb glowing slightly. "I think he's been using it for a while."

McClery swept his flashlight beam over the metal statue, and Jon thought he saw the man visibly sigh in relief.

"You got my message." Frank was staring at Jon in

disbelief. It was the first time they'd seen each other in almost two weeks, and Jon realized it was the longest they'd ever been apart. He ran up to his twin and hugged him tightly.

"Of course I did." Jon laughed, and Frank tightened his grip around his brother. "And you got my message."

"All right," Barrett barked, pulling the boy's attention away from each other, "we need to get him to the medical center." Putting one arm under the boy's legs and the other behind his back, he picked Braydon up.

"Jonny, hold this." McClery handed Jon his cane as he removed his coat and wrapped the guardian in it tightly. "All right, it's safe to hold." He gave it to Jon, who tucked it under his arms. "As for the rest of you"—he glared at Frank and their friends—"we'll talk about this later. Let's get you all home."

It took longer to get back to the medical center than it had to reach Braydon. McClery had overextended his leg and needed to walk more slowly, so Jon held his teacher's arm while he used his cane to beat back the tangled undergrowth. After what felt like hours, they emerged from the forest.

"All of you go to the medical center, and I'll speak with you there shortly," McClery said. His tone left no room for argument.

On their way, Frank and their friends animatedly filled Jon in on all their investigations, their plan to sneak out, and what had happened when they'd confronted Braydon. To Jon, it sounded like a fantastic adventure; he was sorry to have missed most of it.

"You guys did all that for me?" Jon said, a grin pulling at his lips.

"Of course! We'd do anything for Frank's brother," Mira teased, and they all laughed.

Once inside the center, Barrett ordered them to wait in a corner down the hall from where Braydon was placed. The group sat on a couple beds until Professor Mortensen swept in, moving fast. Following at a slower pace was Professor McClery.

"Children!" Mortensen knelt in front of them, touching each of their faces. "Everyone OK?"

Nods went around the group. McClery pulled up a chair for Mortensen, then a second one for himself.

"Good, now tell me everything. What happened? How did you all get into the woods past curfew?" Mortensen was half-dressed in his pajamas, his school sweater thrown haphazardly over the top.

Jon watched the guilt spread over his friends faces, and he smirked. For once, he wasn't involved in the shenanigans.

Mira spoke first, admitting to using her abilities to read the note from Jon. Frank then admitted to using his abilities to read his classmates' minds without permission, which had led them to Braydon. Nate admitted his part in planning to sneak out, and Damien admitted to using his abilities to locate Braydon and the guardian.

"We surrounded him," Frank explained, "but I realized there was something wrong. Braydon needed help. Damien ran back to the school, but I knew he wouldn't make it. So I called for help and—"

"I got Frank's message in my sleep," Jon interrupted.

"Really?" Professor Mortensen's eyes widened. "Are you telling me, Frank, that you sent a message telepathically?"

"I'm really sorry, Professor. I just wanted to get help. I know I'm not suppo—"

"No, Mr. Reed, it's all right. I'm just very impressed."

"He probably saved Mr. Burke's life," Barrett chimed in, appearing behind them. Everyone immediately gave him their attention, anxious for news. "He's doing OK. We're lucky there's no permanent brain damage. The guardian's power is not meant for telepaths. It can have fatal side effects. I put him into a recovery sleep, and he'll be that way for several hours. I hate to think what would have happened if these students hadn't been in the woods tonight."

"I see." Professor Mortensen considered the crew in front of him. "What am I going to do with you all?"

"Maybe start by taking this back"—Jon handed the wrapped-up guardian to Mortensen—"before I'm charged with taking it again."

"Jonathan . . ." Mortensen sighed and took a deep breath. "It's a relief to have this back. It will go into the safe tonight. There will need to be changes to our security if the statue is to live in the Sanctuary again."

"Sir, are we in real big trouble?" Nate asked cautiously.

"We'll talk about that later. For now, I want you all to return to your houses and go to sleep. It's been a long night for all of us. Liam, if you wouldn't mind?" Mortensen held up the guardian, and McClery took it from him.

To Jon's surprise, Mortensen decided to walk them to their houses, dropping off Mira first and then the boys. Amid delight and cheers, he also announced Jon could stay the night at Aries house. "Now, please do as you're told and go to bed" were his last words to the boys before they ran inside and up to their room.

As much as Jon loved being back in his own bunk, he didn't sleep well. No one did. He wanted to hear everything that had happened since he'd been gone, and Frank and his friends were more than happy to share. It was around one in the morning when they finally fell asleep.

∩∩

The next day, they were all called to Professor Mortensen's office. Mira was waiting for them on the bench outside his door when they arrived. Her eyebrows quirked, and she shot a pointed glance at the door as a raised voice escaped from inside.

"I guess he isn't ready for us," Jon whispered as they all took a seat.

"You can't just let them go without consequences for their actions, Richard!" the voice said.

"I'm the superintendent of this school. I will choose the judgment," Mortensen calmly replied.

"Well, I think suspension is necessary. For all, but most of all those Reed boys. They were the instigators."

"Oh, really? Instigators of what?" Now Mortensen's voice rose too. "Returning the guardian to safekeeping or saving a boy's life? I'm having trouble deciding which is more horrific."

"They were outside at night wandering the forest grounds and abusing their gifts."

"Everything they did was to help someone." Mortensen's voice became stern. "I listened to your advice once before, Thurman, and I shouldn't have. For all the misdemeanors I've seen from students, I have yet to expel a student for using their gift to save another person's life or reputation."

"Well, I see now your true colors. So, this is the man who is running this school. I will speak to the board about this. I thought I could trust you, Richard."

The pause that followed lasted almost a full minute.

"I don't think I care to be in your circle of trust, Mr. Thurman. Now, please leave my office."

After another moment of silence, the door opened, and an scowling Mr. Thurman tumbled out. He stared at the five children before him, shoved his hat back on his head, and grunted as he stormed down the hall.

Professor Mortensen came out after him, straightening his blazer before ushering the group of fifth-graders into his office. "Listen, I will not stand for rule breaking. Leaving your houses at night, practicing your gifts without permission, and sneaking around the school are unacceptable behaviors. You have all made my job very difficult and this decision intensely challenging, but I have come to judgment for all of you—except you, Mr. Jonathan Reed, surprisingly."

Frank peeked at his brother, who smirked.

Mortensen took a deep breath, then glanced at the nervous group with a small smile. "You'll have a weeklong shift in the kitchen after dinner each night with Mrs. Sniffens."

That was it? Frank's eyebrows nearly hit the top of his forehead, and Mira smiled.

"Now, with that said, I also want to apologize for your treatment over the last couple of weeks. It's been a challenging time for us all."

Frank rolled his eyes and glanced at Jon. His brother

shrugged. It was probably the only official apology they would get.

"You have all your previous freedoms back. As for your friend Mr. Burke, I heard he's woken up, and I thought you might want to talk to him."

They all nodded, and Mortensen led the way to the medical center. Nurse Barrett and Professor McClery met them at the door.

"He's been asking to speak with Franklin," Barrett said.

Frank's ears perked up. "Why me?"

"Not sure, boy. But you better get in to see him before he falls back asleep," said McClery.

Everyone except Professor Mortensen and Frank waited outside the room. When Frank entered, Braydon was sitting up slightly, his head on a pillow, wiping what looked like tears from his eyes.

"Frank . . ." Braydon said, his voice quiet, "I'm so sorry."

At first, Frank wasn't sure what to say. Braydon had let Jon take the heat for stealing the guardian, even when Jon was threatened with being expelled.

"Braydon, why?" It was the only question he really needed answered.

"I've been sad . . . really depressed." Braydon stared at his hands, tears lingering in his eyes.

"I know," Frank said. In class, there had been several

occasions when Frank had read very sad thoughts and images in Braydon's mind.

"I lost my parents last year." Braydon swallowed. "Car accident. I just wanted to forget about it for a while. The guardian did that for me."

"But why did you take it? How did you even know what it was?"

Braydon's eyes got big, and he looked from Frank to Mortensen with a bit of fear. "I promise you, I didn't take it," he said. "I know what it looks like. But I didn't. I found it."

"You found it?" Mortensen said, sounding skeptical.

Sitting up a little, Braydon ran a hand through his hair. "I was taking out the trash in Gemini house. When I went to put the bag in the trash can, something shiny caught my eye, and there it was. I pulled it out and took it into the woods to play with. I didn't know what it was. Then everyone was getting searched, and I got scared. I panicked. I found a hollow tree stump that the guardian fit into without any trouble, and I shoved leaves over it. I thought they would find it on their search, but they didn't.

"I wanted to give it back, but I was scared after seeing how your brother was treated, Frank. And after using it once, I had to use it again." Braydon squeezed his hands into fists and closed his eyes. "For a few minutes a day, I could pretend I was someone else. I could pretend that nothing bad had happened. It would show me images and sounds. I didn't understand them, but I could focus on nothing else while touching it. I'm so sorry, Professor Mortensen. I'm so sorry, Frank. Please tell your brother I'm sorry. When I found out Jon was going to get expelled, I planned to come forward, but I was in too deep after that. You saved me in more than one way. Thank you."

Frank reached over and took Braydon's hand, and the boy's head slowly nodded forward.

Barrett came in and shooed them away. "He needs to sleep now."

As they left the room, Frank looked up at Mortensen. "Professor, if Braydon didn't steal the guardian, who did?"

"That is a good question, Mr. Reed," he replied, his voice cool and scary. "That is a good question."

The Marsh

CHAPTER 24

Going back to class next week was interesting. Jon had been keeping up with his studies while he stayed at McClery's, but one thing he hadn't prepared for was the hushed conversations that followed him in every classroom. Most students he ran into gave him the cold shoulder. Some had heard new rumors based on what happened Wednesday night.

"I heard they attacked a boy," a girl whispered loud enough for Jon to hear. He sighed and shook his head. Rumors were just rumors, and hopefully the school would soon debunk them.

At PE, Frank and Jon were the last ones waiting to be picked. Both the captains looked at each other with raised eyebrows, neither calling Frank or Jon to their lines.

Professor Yang walked onto the field and glared at them. "Is there a problem?"

"No," a team captain said. "All right, you."

He pointed at Frank, and Jon smirked. The team captains were confused because they couldn't tell them apart. What if you got the wrong twin? What if you got the *trouble-making* one?

PE soccer wasn't the same. Jon's heart wasn't in it.

He was grateful his friends and Frank stayed near him his full first week back. After school every day, they would drop by the house to put their backpacks away, but they never chose to stay inside, even during the light April rains.

"We've been cooped up enough," Damien said.

At week's end, Jon took his baseball mitt and ball into the school yard. They played catch for almost an hour before heading to dinner. Mira sat at their table in the cafeteria; the stares from the other students didn't seem to faze her one bit.

"So, if Braydon didn't take the guardian from the Sanctuary, who did and why?" she asked, but no one answered. It was something they were all asking themselves.

∽∾

As May rolled around, talk about the stolen guardian faded. Even the teachers stopped pressing them about it. Although there were still weekly requests for anyone with information to come forward, it almost felt as if Mortensen and the school board didn't care who took it anymore now that it was returned. Frustrated, Frank still kept notes and explored theories with Nate, Damien, Mira, and Jon.

Braydon was released from the medical center a few weeks after the incident. Frank had tried to visit him a couple times, but Nurse Barrett had refused, saying, "He's struggling with a lot right now. Maybe another time?"

"I think what he could really use is a friend," Frank had argued, but it was no use. Nurse Barrett hadn't budged.

When Frank finally saw Braydon again, the boy was packing his bags into the trunk of a car.

Leaving Mira and Jon on the school steps, Frank ran to catch Braydon before he was driven off the school grounds. He tapped the boy on the shoulder just as he'd finished loading his last suitcase. "No, Braydon! Where are you going? Did they expel you?"

Braydon turned toward him, his head slightly bowed, a small smile on his face. "Hey, Frank. No, I didn't get expelled. The school board was good to me after Nurse Barrett spoke with them. I just need to be with family right now. I have an uncle in Canada who's going to take me in before the school is out. He's a telepath too and told the school he was willing to tutor me. I just . . ." Braydon sighed and ran a hand through his hair. "Thank you, Frank. I know we didn't spend much time together, but you were always nice to me, and I appreciate it. I'm hoping by next year, I'll be ready to come back to school."

"I'll be here when you get back." Frank reached his hand out, and Braydon shook it before turning to get into the car.

Frank's stomach clenched as he watched the car drive away. He didn't know what it was like to lose a family member, but he couldn't imagine not having his mom and dad in his life.

A hand touched his shoulder, and Frank turned to see Mira looking at him with warmth in her eyes. "Secret Valley?"

The suggestion was well received, and the three of them rushed to the trail leading to their hideaway.

"Do you think we should tell Nate and Damien about this place?" Frank asked.

"Nah." Jon dove down on the slide. "Not today!"

After an hour throwing rocks from the statue's outstretched hands, they settled into a relaxed state.

"Seeing Braydon reminded me, what happened to the guardian, Jon?" Mira asked, slouched against the statue's metal thigh.

"I don't know." Jon was sitting on the statue's arms, swinging his legs. "McClery says it's not being kept at the Sanctuary of Knowledge right now. They still don't know how the last person got in."

"At least they don't think you did it anymore," Frank said.

"I think Mr. Thurman still does. I ran into him the other day. You should have seen the look he gave me." Jon stood up on the statue's hand and lifted his arms toward the sky. "I don't care though. I'm free and enjoying it. You hear that, world?" Jon yelled. "I'm free!"

"And annoying!" Mira laughed.

Frank sighed contentedly as he watched his brother from the ground. He was happy—happy to have his brother back, to be in the Secret Valley with Mira, to be free to run around the school again.

Braydon had lost so much and was so sad. Shouldn't Frank feel guilty for being happy? There wasn't an easy answer. He could ask Jon, but Jon wasn't the most empathetic person. He thought about Damien, then realized who he wanted to talk to most was Mom. Mom would know just what to say. She always did.

Frank lay down on his back. Only a month or so until summer break—until home.

∩⌒

Washington was a weird state. It was almost nine o'clock at night, and still the sun shone through their windows into their bedroom. Mira had told Jon that May through August, the sun would stay out until almost ten. This new discovery didn't help Jon's sleeping patterns.

Restless sleep had been the norm for Jon for weeks now. First, it was because of his nightmares, then the theft, and now the nightmares had returned.

Jon watched the sunset from his bunk as he tried to get comfortable. Images kept flashing through his mind, even when his eyes were barely closed. He grumbled and tossed, trying desperately to get to sleep.

He finally drifted off a few hours later, but it didn't last. A pair of hands grabbed at his pajama shirt and tugged, jolting him awake. Eyes shooting open, Jon gripped the intruder's hands and growled.

"It's me!" a frantic voice whispered.

Jon rubbed his eyes, and Frank's blurry face fell into place. "Why'd you wake me?"

Frank released Jon's shirt. "You were grumbling again in your sleep."

"Sorry, Frank. Is everyone else asleep?" Frank nodded, and Jon glanced around the room for confirmation.

A loud *thump* outside their door made them both jump.

"What was that?" Frank asked, but Jon didn't answer. He just threw back his blanket and leaped off his bunk. Stepping lightly to their door, Jon opened it to peek into the hall. At that moment, Levan walked by.

"Levan?" Jon whispered, stepping out of the room. Levan kept walking toward the stairs, and the boys followed. "Wait, Levan, did you hear something too?"

No response.

Jon was whispering but not very quietly; surely Levan had heard him. With his mouth hanging open, Jon watched his friend head down the stairs in his pajamas, turn the corner, open the front door, and stand, eerily still, in the door frame.

"What's he doing?" Frank asked, but Jon was already on the move. A short sprint brought him to Levan's side.

"Levan?" Jon grabbed the head boy's arm. It was limp, swinging loosely against his side once Jon released it. Jon tried waving a hand in front of Levan's open eyes to get his attention, but he didn't so much as blink. "He's zombified! I think he's sleepwalking."

With a blank stare, Levan started to walk into the cool night air. Jon tried to hold him back, but the much larger and stronger boy easily pulled out of his grip. "I can't stop him."

"Then let's get help." Frank gestured toward Professor Yang's room.

But Jon hesitated. Levan was getting farther and farther away from the house. Soon he'd be completely out of sight . . .

"You do that. I'll follow him!" Jon said, pulling on his boots despite Frank's protests. He stepped outside and ran toward the main school building, following Levan.

Jon tried to gather his thoughts as he ran. Somewhere he'd heard you shouldn't wake a sleepwalker, though he didn't remember why. He guessed the only thing he could do was make sure his friend wasn't alone.

At the stairs to the main building, Jon's eyes got big as Levan—in his dazed state—pulled out a ring of keys and unlocked the front door.

Did head students get keys to the school? Confused, Jon followed Levan inside. The building was dark and empty except for the ghostly figure of Levan heading down the hall. He stopped in front of Professor Mortensen's office, pulled out the same set of keys, and unlocked the door.

Jon slowly approached the office after him, but he grabbed the doorframe for support when he saw what Levan was doing within.

The older boy was standing behind Mortensen's desk, staring intensely at a framed blueprint of the school grounds. He raised one hand, and the frame swung open on its own with an eerie *creak*, revealing a hidden wall safe.

Levan rotated his fingers, and the safe's knob moved in sync with the motion. For a minute or so, Jon was mesmerized by Levan's gift of telekinesis, but he was snapped out of it by a soft *click*. The safe was open.

Levan was breaking into the school safe.

Jon rushed into the hall to see if help had arrived yet, but no one was there. His heart started to race as he heard the sound of a door closing behind him.

Jon almost cried out when he turned around.

Towering over him, so close he could almost feel his breath, was Levan, and floating in the air above his head was the Guardian of Whispers.

Levan was still staring off into the distance unsettlingly. He moved forward as if to pass Jon, but Jon put a hand out to stop him, grabbing his nightshirt. To Jon's horror, the boy's vacant eyes peered down on him.

"Stop, Levan, wake up!" Jon shouted, shaking his friend.

Levan's hand shot forward onto Jon's chest. His stare was no longer distant; it was burning into him. His face was barely recognizable—changed into something dark.

Jon shivered. He felt as if the air had been sucked out of his lungs.

"Leave us," Levan growled, but the voice was unfamiliar—animal-like and husky. With a powerful shove, Levan sent Jon sailing through the air. His body slammed against a wall across the hallway, and when he dropped to the ground.

Levan left him, strolling through the front door, down the stairs, and toward the forest.

Through waves of nausea and dizziness, a rush of images hit Jon's mind as he slouched against the wall. A clearing.

Levan was standing in the center, another man beside him.

Frank's face wobbled into his line of sight. "Jon! You OK? What happened?"

He must have blacked out for a moment. Sitting up, he rubbed the back of his sore head, one arm wrapped tenderly around his torso.

"No time for that now. Help me up. We have to catch up to him." Jon grabbed his brother's hand to stand, then dragged him outside.

Professor Yang ran over to them as they walked down the stairs. "Jon? Where is Levan?" Her eyes traveled down to where Jon was awkwardly holding his chest. "What happened?"

"Professor, Levan isn't himself. I just watched him steal the guardian."

Frank gasped, and Yang shook her head.

"That's impossible." She ran up the stairs and into the building to see for herself.

"Professor, he went this way!" Jon tried to stop her, but she was already gone. "Come on, Frank, we have to find him. I think I know which way."

With Frank right behind him, Jon ran, ignoring the stabbing pain in his ribs. They headed into the forest from the school's east side. The old trail led down to the river, and from there, Jon knew they wouldn't have to go far.

Shadow visions were appearing to him one after another, showing him where to go. His head was pounding, but he forced himself to stay alert, to keep trailing through the forest. Before long, they reached the edge of a clearing. It looked familiar, but no one was there. No Levan, no man.

"We must have gotten here before them," Jon said.

Frank leaned his hands on his knees to catch his breath. "Then we should find a place to hide and wait for them." He started walking into the clearing. "Be careful, Jon. It's real muddy through this swamp."

"Swamp?" Jon asked, his voice cracking slightly. Stepping out into the clearing, he felt the soft ground under his boots.

An involuntary shiver ran down his spine, and he unconsciously rubbed his arms and hands. A heavy fog over the clearing's ground had prevented him from noticing it was a marsh.

A marsh, just like his dream. Jon's mouth went dry, and he froze in place.

"Jon, where's your coat?" Frank asked.

"What?" The question shocked him out of his thoughts. *Those words . . .*

"Come on, let's go." Frank waved and kept walking. Jon followed reluctantly. Unlike his dream, his feet didn't sink into the ground; his boot traveled along the soaked earth unhindered.

Halfway into the clearing, Jon's nerves broke. "Frank!"

His brother turned around.

"Whatever happens, don't leave me. Please."

Frank dropped back to him, his brows furrowed. "You OK, Jon? I've never seen you like this."

"Frank, my dream," Jon whispered, his teeth chattering. "This is it. Don't leave me."

"I'm not going to leave you. Now, let's keep going."

Jon nodded, and Frank turned away. This wasn't his dream; things were different. McClery said there were many unknowns in the future, many possibilities.

This idea improved Jon's strength. He started to walk, then discovered he couldn't. His boots—oh, his darn boots! They'd found a sinking spot in the marsh, and they were suctioned into the thick mud below. "Frank, wait! I'm stuck!"

At his brother's shout, Frank turned around, and his eyes widened, staring at a spot above Jon's head. "Jon, behind you!"

As Jon tried to turn, something wrapped around his neck.

"You wretched boy," a venomous voice hissed into his ear, "you and your interfering brother are done making a mess out of my plans."

The grasp on Jon's throat tightened, and he stabbed his nails into the arm of whoever was behind him. Where was Frank? Had he left him? For a moment, Jon felt the sharp sting of betrayal, but then he spotted Frank to his left, losing a battle against Levan. The older boy was wrestling his brother roughly to the ground.

With a burst of anger, Jon did the only think he could think of—bite down on the arm of his captor. The man shouted in pain, and Jon took the opportunity to elbow him under his ribs. With a growl, the man spun Jon around to face him, pulling him completely free of his trapped boots. But the struggle made Jon stumble in the mud, and he fell backward onto his rear.

Groaning, Jon gripped his torso again and stared at the large dark figure hovering above him. "Mr. Thurman?"

Thurman glared down at him. From his bag, he pulled out the guardian, wrapped in a handkerchief. "You know how long I've been trying to get my hands on this? I would have had it months ago if the first plan hadn't failed. I really thought it was you who took it from me." He snapped his fingers, and Levan appeared at his side, pulling along a muddy and worn Frank. "There." He pointed, and Levan tossed Frank down next to Jon.

"Why do you want it?" Jon asked as the man held the guardian up to admire it.

"You'd wonder why, wouldn't you? You have the gift everyone wants but can't have, Reed. Maybe I want to see the future."

"But you're a psychic," Jon said, his courage rising. Glancing over to check on his brother, Jon saw he had his eyes closed and that his lips were moving in a near-silent murmur. *Good, Frank, call for help!* Maybe Jon could buy his brother some time. "I thought each person has only one gift."

Thurman huffed at him. "If I have only one gift, how do you suppose I keep Mr. Mason here under control? You know so little about all this. There's much they don't want you children to know." The tall, sickly man turned to Levan and sneered. "I don't need you anymore."

With a snap of Thurman's fingers, Levan collapsed to the ground.

"No! What did you do to him?" Jon asked.

"He'll be fine. He won't even remember anything. You two, on the other hand . . . I can't have you telling anyone. You'll need some memory adjustments as well." He smiled. "I do need to test this out."

Tossing away the handkerchief from the guardian, Thurman closed his eyes and gripped the statue tightly. Jon's head began burning from the inside as the guardian's small orb started to glow. He'd never seen that happen when he used the artifact. Shadow figures billowed from the guardian in a cloud of smoke—growing larger, surrounding Thurman, then spreading over the area where Jon and Frank were sitting. Pain exploded behind Jon's eyes, and he grabbed his brother's hand.

"Frank!" Jon cried as Thurman's eyelids shot open, revealing only the whites of his eyes. The man tilted his chin down to look at them, walking forward with deliberate steps. Small bursts of electricity sparked from the guardian as he raised it over their heads.

"I've never felt so much power, so much uncontrolled energy," he whispered, sounding crazed. "This is more than I could have hoped for, maybe even the key to everything."

"I got you, Jon!" Frank gripped Jon's shirt as Thurman reached a hand toward him.

The pain in Jon's head overwhelmed the pain in his ribs, and he curled into himself, screaming.

A Battle

CHAPTER 25

Thurman's hand stopped inches from Jon's head, as if something was holding him back.

"Who is doing this?" he growled. His ghastly mouth twisted into a snarl as his sunken white eyes searched the clearing.

"I am." Professor Yang stepped out of the shadow smoke, her hands outstretched.

"You can't hold me by yourself, Yang. I am more powerful than you know."

Jon watched as the two pushed mentally back and forth. Thurman seemed to be wiggling out of her grasp, the arm with the guardian beginning to inch forward.

"No, she can't do it alone," another voice said from the darkness, "but we can do it together!" Levan stepped up from behind Thurman, his arms stretched out like his teacher's, and the guardian tore from the man's grasp and flew into Levan's hands. He dropped it quickly, as if it were blazing hot. Yang took advantage of the distraction to bind Thurman in a tighter hold, keeping her focus on him as the smoke dissipated.

"Min?" a voice called from forest.

"Over here!" she shouted back.

The horizon seemed to move and sway as a group of teachers trampled in their direction. Finally released from the guardian and Thurman's hold, Jon's vision started to blacken around the edges. The relief of unconsciousness hit him just as his mentor's face appeared over his head, asking him a question he could no longer hear.

∩⌒

Frank was covered in mud from head to toe, his clothing was sticking to him in all sorts of embarrassing places, and he couldn't stop shivering. But none of that mattered as he watched McClery lean over his brother, concern etched onto his face.

"He's OK, Franklin," the man assured him as Mortensen reached down to pick up Jon. "Be careful with him, Richard." McClery offered a hand to Frank and helped him stand. "Come on, let's get out of the cold and cleaned up."

Professor Owens put a hand on Thurman's forehead, and the man instantly went limp. Yang caught him in midair and carefully led the way back to the school with his floating form in tow. Levan, wobbly on his feet, was helped along by Nurse Barrett, and Professor Vidra followed with a nicely wrapped-up guardian in her arms.

After being checked by another medical center staff person, Frank was instructed to shower, change, and stay under a warm blanket. His arms and face felt bruised, as if he'd been in a hard soccer match. Levan was a junior in high school and much larger than Frank. Their wrestling had left him sore. At least the shiver was almost gone. The blanket and shower had taken the chill away.

When he was finally allowed to see Jon, his brother had already been cleaned up, and Nurse Barrett was wrapping a bandage around his ribs. Frank's nose wrinkled at the sight of the large bruise around Jon's neck, as well as the many other dark places on his arms and chest. Though Frank thought he looked terrible, Jon was awake and smiling as he walked up.

"No need to worry, nothing's broken," Nurse Barret was saying. "But you did slightly bruise a rib. You'll need to take it easy. I know that's hard for a ten-year-old boy." He laughed

"Thank you," Jon said as Barrett moved over to check on Levan.

"This should warm you up." Professor Yang brought over a tray of hot cocoa, and Frank settled into the chair by Jon's bed, taking the warm drink in his hands.

"I don't remember anything really," Levan said from the bed across from them, his head in his hands, "just dreams."

Professor Owens was sitting in a chair beside him. "It will take time for those memories to come back, Mr. Mason. We'll need to work on it together. It won't be easy."

"I don't care. I need to know what happened." The boy's wild eyes peeked through his fingers, glancing over at the twins.

Frank looked the other way, not sure how to react. In many ways, Frank owed Levan his and Jon's life. He had stopped Thurman before something horrible happened to them. But he'd also hurt them both.

"Levan, let's just rest for now," Owens said. "We'll need to take this process slow."

The older boy nodded, and Frank noticed how tired and beat up Levan appeared; several bruises darkened his arms and face. Frank stretched his back and winced. He probably looked similar from their tussle.

Jon was still shivering, but McClery appeared almost out of nowhere and dropped a large warm blanket on his shoulders, smirking. "Come on, boys, let's give your friend some privacy." He guided them to a small exam room down the hall, and Frank and Jon slumped onto the examination bed. "I know you're both tired, but I doubt Mortensen will let you go back to your houses without a statement."

"What will happen to Levan?" Jon asked, staring into his cocoa.

"Not sure," McClery said. "For now, why not get some rest. I'll wake you when we need you."

Frank had been rubbing his eyes, and Jon stifled a yawn. Together, they lay down on the small bed, Jon's blanket wrapped around them.

Jon fell asleep instantly, and Frank watched him for some time before his eyelids grew too heavy to keep open. His mind started to drift in and out of sleep. Words and memories from the evening tossed about in his mind like restless ocean waves.

Whatever happens, don't leave me, a desperate voice shouted.

"Never," Frank mumbled as he slipped into a heavy slumber.

∩⌒

When Jon finally woke, it took him a few moments to realize he was still in the medical exam room. Frank was snoring on the small bed they shared, and Jon was crushed up against him, an arm around his shoulders.

Shrugging off his sleeping twin, he slipped off the bed

and onto the cold linoleum floor, glancing at the clock. Noon. They'd slept the whole morning away.

Jon heard hushed voices outside the exam room, and he stretched and opened the door. Several teachers stood in a circle a few yards down the hall, and as he approached, they stopped talking.

"Is it Jonathan or Franklin?" Mortensen asked.

"That's Jonny," McClery said next to him.

Yang checked her watch. "I need to get back to my house."

"I'll walk with you," Owens offered.

Nurse Barrett moved farther down the hall to check on Levan, and Professor Mortensen approached Jon, backing him up into the room where Frank still slept. McClery was right behind him.

"Let's talk, Mr. Reed."

"Is Levan OK?" Jon settled on the bed, his voice low so as not to wake Frank.

Mortensen wiped a hand down his face. "Your friend has been through a lot."

"I don't know how, Professor, but Levan wasn't himself when he took the guardian. I watched him. It was like he was under a spell."

"We know. Professor Owens was able to work through a repressed memory of tonight's events. There is no doubt

Levan was being controlled by Thurman. Tonight and . . ." He paused and then sighed loudly. ". . . and before."

"What?" Jon's eyes widened, and his mouth dropped open. "Before?

"Jonathan, it was Thurman after the guardian the whole time. I don't know why or what exactly happened tonight, but Levan wasn't in control of his actions when Thurman used him to steal the guardian the first time."

"If that's true, why did Thurman get so mad at me?" Jon thought back to the suspicious looks and mean accusations. "He thought I had it!"

"I think that's because he thought you actually did have it."

"What do you mean?"

"Jonny, you remember that night you saw a shadow person sneaking around the school?" McClery asked, and Jon nodded. "You stayed out late, but they never showed up? It was the night of the theft. My guess is you saw Levan's future self in that shadow. He was trying to take the guardian to Thurman. However—"

"However," Mortensen cut McClery off, "Owens and I both read that you disrupted the plan by hanging out at the school. Thurman had to hide the guardian and planned to retrieve it later."

"The garbage can!" Jon shouted, and Frank groaned

behind him.

"Yes, where I believe Braydon found it."

"Where Braydon found what?" Frank said as he sat up.

They took a few minutes to catch Frank up, then Jon asked what would happen to Levan.

"No punishment will be given to Levan. He didn't have control over the situation. Thurman is the criminal for not only stealing the guardian but breaking society rules. Controlling someone's mind is illegal, with life imprisonment as a judgment—although there aren't many people who have mastery level like that. I've known Thurman for over twenty years. Lately, he hasn't been himself. I had no idea he had such skills. He isn't a telepath." Mortensen's face lost color as he spoke.

"Perhaps he had someone helping him," McClery added.

The superintendent sighed. "Let's hope we caught the right person. I would hate to think this isn't over."

"Now, boys," McClery said, "tell us what happened to you."

The boys quickly ran through their version of what happened, telling the story together.

"Then I kicked Levan in the knee to get him off me." Frank acted out the moment. "Jon was on the ground with Thurman, who had the guardian in his hands."

"It was like my dream, Liam!" Jon said, and Mortensen

raised an eyebrow at him. "I mean, Mr. McClery. Just like the one I told you. Well, almost exactly like it—the fog, the mist, and the mushy ground. I froze!"

"This event is strongly attached to your feelings and energy. I'm not surprised it's been haunting your sleep for so long," McClery said. "What else did you see?"

"Shadows and smoke. It came from the guardian, and Thurman seemed possessed."

"I didn't see any shadows or smoke," Frank said with a frown.

McClery rubbed his chin. "Interesting."

"What do you think that means?" Mortensen asked him.

"Jonny's flash visions are made of shadows and forms. This 'smoke' from the guardian could mean several different things. In many ways, an oracle mind is attached to oracle objects. We can see things others cannot, because these objects are sensitive to our presence. That's probably why it had such an adverse reaction to Thurman—probably also why you blacked out, Jonny."

"You too were impressive, Franklin," Mortensen added. "Your telepathic message woke up both me and Nurse Bennet. We were able to trace where you were. You perform well under pressure."

Frank blushed, and Jon laughed.

"You both were very brave," Mortensen stated. "I'm

just grateful you're safe. I called your family while you were asleep. Your parents are anxious to talk to you both."

A warmth spread through Jon's chest at the mention of talking with his parents. "Professor McClery, do you think the dreams will stop now?" He hoped they would.

"I think that dream will stop. Will there be others?" McClery shrugged. "I don't know. But I think without the dreams, you wouldn't have been prepared to fight off Thurman."

"Where is he, anyway?" Jon asked. "Mr. Thurman, I mean?"

"He's already been taken away to be tried for his crimes," Mortensen said, to Jon's relief. "I'm very sorry for what you two went through in this situation—especially you, Jonathan. What can I do to make this right?"

Jon looked over at Frank with a smile. "I think we have an idea."

The Last Match

CHAPTER 26

The twins were released from the society investigators only to share the story again with their friends at dinner that night. The stares Jon and Frank got from the students around them made them laugh.

"I think you have more bruises than me," Jon teased Frank.

"At least visible ones."

"Attention! Attention! Can I have everyone's eyes up here?" Professor Mortensen said to the cafeteria, and talking fizzled out. "I just wanted to let you all know, the real thief of the guardian has finally been caught. I would also like to stop the rumors that this thief was a student." A flurry of whispering broke out, and a few students gasped in shock. "The school board and I would like to send out an apology to all unjustly accused parties. They would also like to send a special thanks to the Aries fifth-grade boys and Mira Camacho for the brave return of the guardian to its home."

At the end of his speech, Mortensen winked at the twins, and the eyes of every West Hills student turned to their table.

"Yes!" Damien said too loudly, pumping a fist in the air. When everyone at the table stared at him, he ducked his head low with a small smile. "Sorry."

Over the rest of May and into June, the attitude of Frank's schoolmates had a different temperament towards him and his friends. At various times throughout the day, he got pats on the back and high fives from students he didn't even know. Everyone in class wanted to be their partner in science and or sit at their table at lunch to hear what happened.

"Go away! Can't you see we are trying to eat in peace here!" Mira had shouted at an annoyingly close group of students at the table. The student's dispersed and Damien longingly looked at them. "They aren't trying to be your friend Damien. They just want to know what happened. We're like a tourist attraction!"

"I know." Damien said as he bit into his sandwich.

Levan had returned to classes after a week in the medical center with Professor Owens and Yang. Levan seemed almost himself except he didn't resumed his head boy duties. At least not yet. It wasn't common knowledge in the school that Levan had taken the guardian and they, Jon and Frank, had vowed they would never tell.

By mid-June, excitement over the guardian had cooled down, and the last soccer match of the season was the new hot topic. The final was between the Gemini-Sagittarius team and the Cancer-Pisces team, which had both been undefeated all season.

The day of the match was sunny and cloudless. For the first time since holiday break, Frank didn't have to wear his jacket outside. The temperature had climbed to eighty degrees, and everyone but the boys complained about the heat. Nate had even gone so far as to dumped it on his head.

"I would never survive Florida…" he whined. "I don't know how you do it."

"Where is your home town Nate?" Frank asked.

"Alaska!" Nate laughed as Frank's eyes got big. He couldn't imagine the temperatures there but if it was anything like TV, it was cold. "You'll have to visit someday."

"No thank you."

At the field, the metal benches were filling up as students from every house came to support their favored teams. The Gemini Sagittarius team fans wore yellow and purple while Cancer Pisces fans sported their best light green and silver colors. While Frank could find nothing wear for the occasion he was just happy to watch the match. Since Aries house hadn't made the final competition, they could choose whomever they wanted to root for.

"I'll just root for the winner," Damien told them as they settled into a row.

"How are you going to cheer if you don't know who wins until the end?" Nate asked.

Damien smirked. "It's easy. When a team gets a goal, I'll root for them, and if the other team gets two goals, I'll root for them. So, whoever is in the lead."

"Oh brother! That's the worst way to choose." Nate shook his head.

Frank ended up picking the Cancer-Pisces team at the last minute. Each team played well, and Frank's voice got hoarse from cheering. It came down to the last few minutes, with the teams tied at one to one.

Beside him, Mira was on the edge of her seat, Jon was standing to shout, and Damien wasn't sure which team to cheer for.

On the field, a girl with long wavy hair swept into a ponytail was whipping past players from the Gemini-Sagittarius team. Frank cheered, his feet tapping the bench in excitement as she dribbled down the field. As she neared the goal, a defender closed in on her.

But with a swift kick, she knocked the ball into the air and toward the opposing team's goalie. Everyone in the stands jumped to their feet to watch. The ball was heading straight into the upper goal corner, the hardest place for the goalie to reach. Frank held his breath, and then gasped as the ball was redirected in midair just enough to bounce off the goal.

"What?" the fans shouted.

"That's not fair!" Nate yelled, his fist in the air. A whistle blew and Professor Yang in her referee uniform came to the penalty box.

"Alright, which one of you did it?" She glared around the field and pointed to the Gemini-Sagittarius players. "I know which of you are telekinetic. Sham and Addie, come forward."

"It was me." A player stepped up and admitted. Half the fans booed while the other half was quiet. Yang pulled out a red card and handed it to the player, who nodded and left the field.

"How do they handle it when people cheat with their gifts?" Frank whispered to Jon, and his brother shrugged. But soon their question was answered as Yang set up for a penalty shot. The Cancer-Pisces player positioned herself at the goal and, at the whistle, took a good shot. It wasn't as good as her first one, but it still slipped past the goalie, and the player's teammates rushed her for a hug.

The game ended with Cancer-Pisces winning two to one. It was the most interesting soccer game Frank had ever watched.

"How are we going to go back to watching regular soccer without gifts?" He laughed.

During the last week of term, teachers started piling on homework again. Science with Professor Gonzalez and math with Professor Wyatt were particularly brutal.

Frank and Jon studied together for exam week. PE had already ended, so each day consisted of just one test. Math was on Monday, science on Tuesday, English next, then social science, and their gift test on Friday. The gift tests were scheduled early in the morning, giving students time to pack for summer break.

Walking into his classroom on Friday, Frank wasn't surprised to find he wasn't taking a traditional test.

"Your goal is to answer the questions on your test based on how your partner across from you would answer them. You will do this by telepathy only. There will be no talking, no gesturing, only silence. Any student caught cheating will get an automatic F. Now begin." Professor Owens let them work in silence for almost an hour.

When the test ended, each student passed their paper to their partner to grade. It felt weird grading another student's paper, but his test partner had done well. He'd only missed a couple questions: Frank's favorite comic was Wolverine, not Spiderman, and his favorite food was spaghetti, not macaroni.

After they turned in their test, everyone rushed back to their houses to celebrate. Some students tore off their school vests and swung them above their heads in excitement.

It didn't take long for Jon to run up and hug Frank when he got back to Aries house. "Franky! We get to go home!" Jon only called him Franky when he was in a really good mood. The last day of school brought big grins to all the students.

Frank was packed and ready to go early. After Levan inspected their meticulously cleaned room and told them they were good to go, they ran out to see Damien and Nate off. Their shuttle was leaving a few hours before Frank and Jon's.

"You'll write, right?" Nate asked.

"I don't know. I didn't write a single letter to my parents the whole time I was here," Jon said.

"I'll write Nate," Frank told him.

The twins stayed on the curb until the van pulled away.

No more than an hour later, it was time to say goodbye to Mira. Her father had pulled his car up the school driveway to pack her luggage into the back. He greeted both the twins warmly with a wave as Mira attacked them with a long hug.

"You both stay out of trouble. I know it'll be hard without me around." She laughed, despite the tears in her eyes. "Send me some of that Florida sunshine." Receiving their promise that they would, she happily waved to them as the car drove away.

Because their flight was later, Frank and Jon were leaving on the last shuttle of the day. They waited on the Aries house porch, their trunks already loaded into the van, and sat on the porch swing, letting their bare feet dangle.

"I miss them all so much—Mom, Dad, Auntie Gladys, Peter, Clara, and even grumpy Genie." Frank looked over to his brother. Jon was gazing over the school campus. It seemed like a ghost town to Frank now that most students had gone home.

"Frank, do you think we've changed?" Jon asked.

The question took him by surprise, and Frank had to think about it for a moment. It seemed so long ago they'd played soccer in the crabgrass behind their house. It felt like a different time when they'd ridden their bikes through the neighborhood with their friends.

"I don't feel the same anymore. I'm not the same Jon that left home in October."

"Well, we've grown a bit." Frank wasn't really sure what else to say, but he was feeling it too. "We aren't the same. I've seen things, done things, that none of our friends back home could have seen or done. It's going to be hard to see them and know we can't tell them any of it. I mean, look at us. We've been through food fights, regular fights, house arrests, and medical emergencies—not to mention all the crazy things that happened in our gifts classes."

"I know. It's just, I keep thinking about something McClery told me."

"What?"

"'It's not over, Jonny,'" Jon quoted. "'It's all just beginning.' I know I'm supposed to see the future, but I have no idea what he was talking about."

"Maybe he means all the changes that will happen for us as we learn. You know, the new Frank and the new Jon!"

"I just hope our friends back home will like the new Jon." He smirked at his brother, and Frank patted him on the back.

"I don't know. *I* still like you, and that's saying a lot." A honk from the shuttle driver announced to the boys it was time to go. "Come on, bro. Let's go home."

Mr. Unknown

CHAPTER 27

The man hit his arms against the wall of his gloomy cell with an angry shout, crushing the small plastic cup they'd given him in his fist.

How could everything have gone so wrong? Now there was no way to retrieve the artifact—not without getting caught. His fingers clenched, shaking with rage. There had to be a way to get what he was looking for, a way to extract the information he wanted.

If only that boy hadn't found the guardian before he'd gotten there. If only those meddling kids hadn't gotten in the way. If only that arrogant child had been expelled and he'd been given the chance for a proper search . . .

Wait. The arrogant child. That loudmouth troublemaker of a boy could be exactly what he was searching for. Maybe, just maybe, he'd be able to see the future.

He mulled the thought over in his head. Enacting something on that large of a scale would be risky; he would have to be careful, intentional in his actions.

Taking a deep breath, he pulled his fist back and hit the wall with as much force as possible. Vibrating pain radiated down to his elbow, and blood trickled from his knuckles as he yelled through the prison bars. "Guards! Help! I'm hurt!"

The sound of rushing steps made him smirk.

If he was going to pull this endeavor off, he first needed to do one particular thing. Something he'd been hoping to put off for a few more years. As the guard approached, he prepared himself.

It was time for a new face.

The Reed Brothers adventure continues in

The Secrets of Arkaim

About the Author

B.E. Padgett was born and raised in the pacific northwest. She is a proud Washingtonian who grew up in a loud and chaotic family of eight.

Although she enjoys many things in life, she considers being an auntie one of her biggest joys.

B. E. writes fiction that shares the chaos, turmoil, and beauty of large families, especially siblings or chosen family members. She is a member of the Society of Children's Book Writers and Illustrators and author of Reed Brothers Series.

B. E. was a student affairs professional and managed student leadership programs at a community college for ten years. She is dedicated to inclusion, equity, sustainability, and love for everyone.

Hobbies and talents include: crocheting stuffed animals, dress up tea parties, graphic design, illustration, whistling and all things art.

Want to connect with B.E. Padgett? Follow her on:

Facebook: @bepadgettwriting
Twitter: @BEPadgett1
Author Website: www.bepadgett.com

Made in the USA
Columbia, SC
01 December 2021

50204695R00174